Phighter: A Northeast Story
By Danny Montvydas

Foreword

At the time of the publishing of this book, I've known Dan for about a decade. Dan and I met when I joined the scouts in second grade but we were both also on my grade school's swim team, we became great friends and I've considered him as a brother to me ever since. The way in which he describes the main character, Donnie, is roughly how Dan is as a person. A die-hard Eagles fan and Phillies fan right out of the womb, born and raised in Philadelphia. As well as someone who likes to go out and play sports with friends at the rec, whether it's football or baseball.

When Dan came up to me about writing a book, he asked me if I would help him work out some of the details of going to Father Judge since he went to Saint Joe's Prep. To help him out, I gave him my Junior year roster and helped explain what it's like at a day in Judge. After that, he had asked me to be one of his editors, and me wanting to continue to help with what I could, I accepted.

Although I never enjoyed books and still to this day won't read one if I can help it, I would slowly read through the book and point out some things that I noticed. After a while, he had offered me the job of finishing the book and writing the foreword for him since we have known each other for the majority of both of our lives.

If you know the areas of Fox Chase and Holmesburg, you will most likely know where the characters are in the story. The book goes over some of the most well-known areas in these two neighborhoods and the surrounding areas. This book will also cover the main things that most high school students will go through in their high school career: love, heartbreak, grief, disappointment, friendships, and enemies.

I hope all who read the book enjoy it because I know I did.

Kenny Hein

Author's Note

Hey Everyone!

Yeah... This is my book. This is the largest book I've written. I started writing my sophomore year of high school as a way to distract myself from my school work. I remember spending hours straight, staying up till three, sometimes four in the morning multiple nights in a row for around four months. And around Easter my sophomore year, I had fifty Google doc pages of writing and after that, I said to myself "What the heck do I do with this?" So I brought it to my sophomore year English teacher, Mr. Patragnoni. If you're reading this, your class was the bomb. He edited it and talked me through revising it and at the end of all of it, he asked what I wanted to do with it. Quite frankly, I had no idea what I wanted to do with it because I was fifteen and clueless. He told me I should publish it and I agreed with him one hundred percent. But my grades caught up to me. They bit me in the butt a little bit and it didn't even come to my mind again till November of my senior year when I was going through old files. I saw it, read it a few times and just said "Screw it." I self-published my first book at seventeen years old, which has recently been majorly revised and enlarged. I had officially become an author. After that, I just kept writing. It's a great hobby. I recommend anyone that's going through rough times or wants to do something, just write it out. It could be scribbles on a napkin or typing on a Google doc. Writing has always been an excellent way to de-stress. I've written probably around twenty to twenty-five short stories and about two to three other book ideas averaging about forty to fifty pages each that need major, major edits. Nonetheless, it kept me distracted and I love doing it. Around December of 2019 was when I had my idea for this book. It was around two o'clock in the morning and I just thought to myself, "No one writes books about Northeast Philly or sets them in Northeast Philly. I'll write one myself." And I stayed up the whole night, brainstorming ideas for my book. As I wrote it, I had a lot of help from my English teacher of the time, Mr. Coyle, who introduced me to some of my favorites books to date, *Fight Club, Trainspotting* and *Requiem For A Dream*. Most especially, *Requiem For A Dream*, a great book which I drew inspiration from because of the uplift and downfall of the characters, the extreme detail in writing and the setting of the book and the accents seen throughout the book. After three months of writing, I had about sixty Google doc pages of writing and I asked a couple of my close friends to help me edit and just give me general feedback of my book and they were awesome. Beyond helpful. They gave me edits to help with the plot, character development, grammer, everything. Through their help, I was able to get my book to over a

hundred pages long of pure Northeast Philly love with my own creativity placed right at the heart of it. Over the last four months, it's been through edits and revisions a plenty and through talks with my parents and my own research, I decided to publish it through self-publishing. So sit back and enjoy. You'll laugh and you'll cry. This is a story of love and hate. This is a story of uplift and downfall. This is my heart and soul on paper and from the bottom of my heart, I love all of you who chose to read it.
Very Sincerely,

Author Danny Montvydas

I want to thank my Mom and Dad for helping me through this book(and for giving birth to me or whatever). I want to thank my editors but more importantly my friends; Matt Purcell, Matt Lombardi, Michael Ruggiero and Kelly McPoyle for wanting to read this book and helping me out through one of the hardest processes of making a book. Youse guys are the best. I want to thank my best friend, Kenny Hein, for writing my foreword. This kid has been a brother to me for over a decade and I can't wait to spend the next one with him. I want to thank all of my friends who eagerly agreed to be a character when I asked them. I want to thank Jared Williams, who not only took fantastic photos for my book, he's also an awesome kid and a great friend. Finally, I want to thank Mr. Patragnoni and Mr. Coyle, because without them, I wouldn't have had the inspiration nor the willpower to publish my first book and this one as well.

For Thomas "Fish" Bowdren. Fly High Pop-Pop

I

Ugh. School. Starting in a few days. All Donny can do is dread the return.

The workload.

The stress.

Him.

Donny sighs loudly and turns on the music, watching his thoughts fade away and his body become calm, as he's driving home in his little black sedan. He feels the warm August breeze in his hair and cruises Rhawn Street.

Home from soccer practice, he showers and changes.

"Hey Ma, I'm headin out!"

"Where you goin?"

"Over a friends. I'll be back tomorrow mornin."

"Be safe!"

Donald Richard Mooney, born on January fifteenth of the year two thousand, at eight pounds three ounces, has grown up in the beautiful neighborhood of Fox Chase. He's your average Northeast Philly kid, Irish as shit and a lover of sports. A graduate of St. Cecilia's, he goes to Father Judge High School, where he plays soccer and baseball, while smoking too many cigarettes and drinking way too much.

Donny walks out the back door of his house and makes a beeline for his neighbor's bush, where he's hiding a matte-black Jansport backpack. He opens the bag, grinning at the sight of the cans of tea and beer. He zips it up and pulls his phone out of his pocket to text his friend.

'Ey Benny.'

'Ey Wassup Donny.'

'I got the stuff. You picking me up?'

'Yeah, I'm right around the corner. I'll be there in a minute.'

Donny's walking back to the front of his house as he sees his friend pull up. The front tire jumps the curb, and the car jolts upward violently.

"You good?"

"Yea. Hop in!"

Donny slips his book bag off of his back and tosses it into the backseat as the two boys dab each other up.

"Wassup, bro."

"Wassup, Benny."

Benjamin Andrew Kennedy--A white kid so Irish, he sweats Guinness when he works out,--goes by the nickname "Benny" (or "Dipshit" when he's being an idiot), is fun as hell. A heavy drinker and even heavier smoker, he'll make your day. A St. Jerome's graduate, student at Father Judge and an avid baseball player, he'll fuck you up on and off the field. Don't mess with him.

"You got the stuff?"

"Psssh. Do I?"

Donny reaches into the back seat, grabs the bag, and cracks it open. Benny peers in, eyeballing all the booze packed into it.

"It's gonna be fun tonight!"

Donny nods as the boys pull onto Rhawn and cruise down the street, windows down, music making the whole car vibrate. They veer onto Cresco and pull up to Benny's house. After Benny parks the car, they get out and start walking down the street to the trails, heading to Karma, a popular drinking spot in the Pennypack Woods.

There are many spots like these. Trails. Heaven. Unknown. Crater. You name it, Northeast has got it. The boys get into the woods and walk down the trails until they get to the spot, flooded with teenagers. You could see every high school there. Judge, Ryan, Little Flower, Roman, Huberts, Everyone.

Benny's staring down at his phone, looking at his texts, trying to see who's here.

"Whatchu got?"

"Well, just from lookin, Taylor's here. Sarah's here. I think . . ."

Benny's phone buzzes in his hand, and he looks down at a text.

"Yeah, Aidan here's too."

"Well, let's go meet up wit'im."

The two boys walk around, beers in hand, looking for Aidan.

"DONNY!"

The ground seemingly shakes as Aidan walks over to the two boys and dabs them up.

Aidan Daniel Smith. A gargantuan man with a gargantuan heart. Standing at a mere six foot four, he will crush you like a Bud Light can. A lineman for Judge's varsity football team and a St. Albert the Great's graduate, he is a brick wall of flesh and muscle. Nothing gets past him, not even a good time, which makes him a hell of a lot of fun at kegs and parties.

The three boys talk about how their summers went as Donny reaches into his bag, pulling out a beer for Aidan.

"Here ya go, bro."

Aidan nods gratefully as Donny hands him the can.

"Aight guys. Let's go!"

The three boys drink their summers away. All their thoughts of school, thoughts of junior year, thoughts of stress and everything else fade away. Their night's drinking is reinforced by the sheer amount of nicotine coursing through their body for the entirety of the evening. Benny was such a heavy smoker, he'd gotten Donny hooked on it too. Donny's chain-smoking habits somehow went unrecognized by his folks.

Guess he was just sneaky.

At one point, after about four or five cans of beer and a few teas, Donny looks down at his phone, reading quarter past eleven. Maybe it's a quarter past one. Donny doesn't care. It doesn't matter anyway. Sirens ring out through the warm late summer night. Pandemonium ensues as kids are booking it in forty different directions. Cans, bottles, and condom wrappers litter the dirt. Donny starts running but is too far gone, he blacks out, feeling his mind become groggy and his body become limp, his head hitting the dirt a few seconds later.

"Benny?"

Donny wakes up on a couch, shirtless, with scratches covering over his body and a pounding headache.

Benny's staring at the TV in his room, playing on his console. He turns around to Donny and looks at him with a wicked smile.

"Thank God. I thought you died. I was boutta cawl the damn cops."

"What the fuck happened?"

Benny sighs loudly and turns off his TV.

"You blacked out almost immediately as the cops arrived. You couldn't walk. You couldn't tawk. Nuthin. I had to give you a goddamn piggyback ride as we ran outta the woods. We got to the tracks and you woke up but just enough to vomit your brains out and then you passed out again. You threw up on your shirt, your pants, everything. We walked down the tracks till we lost the cops and then walked back to my house, where I had to clean you up. So you're welcome, dickhead."

Donny rubs his eyes and looks over at Benny, whose headset is back on and is staring at the TV again. Donny looks around the room and grabs a piece of paper that's laying on the table behind him. He crumbles it into a ball and tosses it at Benny's head, bouncing off of Benny's crew cut hairstyle.

"Wassup?"

"Got a cig?"

"Yeah. Smoke'em outside though. My rents don't like that crap in here."

Benny reaches into a desk drawer and whips out a pack of Marlboros and tosses it to Donny.

He walks outside to his friend's steps, standing there with no shirt and gray sweatpants tucked into his socks. He places the cancer stick in his mouth and looks at his lighter and flicks it, watching the flame appear seemingly from nowhere. He moves the bright orange flame to the end of the cigarette, watching it burn the paper and the tobacco as he breathes in deeply, feeling the burn of the smoke. The taste smacks him across his hungover face and buries itself deep into his lungs.

He might smoke two. He barely feels it anymore.

He rips through the first cig and is halfway through the second as he sees Benny's parents' car drive up the street. He takes one last quick inhale, flicks the butt into the neighbor's yard, and runs into the house.

"Benny, your rents are home."

Benny immediately turns off the TV and races around the basement, cleaning up the room.

"I thought they weren't supposed to be home till tonight."

"I dunno, dude. Did you check your phone?"

"Damn it!"

Benny walks over and grabs his phone from his backpack, looking at his notifications.

'Hey Benny. The trip ended earlier than expected. We should be home tomorrow morning. Have fun. Don't stay up too late and no parties. See you tomorrow morning.'

"Aw shit."

The two boys manage to semi-clean the room to an OK state, which they consider exceptional, given the circumstances and their severely hung-over state. The two boys, breathing heavily from racing around the room, recline on the couch and put on a movie.

"Good stuff, Donny."

"Good stuff, Benny."

The boys fist-bump as the early morning sun shines through a cloudless sky and in through the basement door.

Yesterday was perfect. Today might be even better.

II

The sound of white plastic whistles through the air as it drops like a dive-bomber from his head to his ankles. Donny watches the ball, holding his grip tightly as the ball soars on the outside. He moves the fluorescent yellow bat forward, yet stops, checking his swing as it curves outside. He looks at the umpire with his eyes staring intently . . .

"STTTRRRIIIKKKEEE THREE! YOU'RE OUT!"

My friend Patty screams from behind the plate as he throws his hands in the air in emulation.

"Aw, come on, Patty, that was three feet off the fuckin plate."

"Cawl's a cawl, Donny, you know that."

Donny rolls his eyes as he smirks at his friend, handing the bright yellow bat off to the next kid. He walks over to the bench to the right of the backstop cage.

Patrick Michael O'Callahan, nicknamed Patty or O'Cal, is one skinny kid. Standing at five foot seven and weighing probably a buck ten soaking wet, Patty is probably the least athletic kid out there. Couldn't run, couldn't catch, couldn't throw. So the neighborhood kids made him the designated umpire/referee whenever they played at the rec and he does a damn fine job at it too. A year younger than Donny but a graduate of Cecilia's as well, he's been friends with Donny since the third grade.

"You'll get'em next time, Donny."

"I hope so. I'm gonna smack the shit outta that pitcher if I get the chance."

His friend taps him on his back as he gets up and goes to cheer on his friends. Donny and a bunch of the neighborhood kids are playing wiffle ball at Sweeney Field, in the beautiful neighborhood of Fox Chase, as the late fall season sets in.

"Ey Shea, can you pass me my wooder?"

His friend Shea, who's cheering on his team, walks over to his bag, grabs it and passes him his bottle. Donny takes a swig from his plastic water bottle and moves down the bench next to his friend.

Seamus Robert Miller, Shea to pretty much everyone, was a hell of a friend and an even better baseball player. His best friend since T-ball. But don't mess with him. Standing at five foot ten with a medium build, he knows how to rumble and he'll rock your shit. A St. Cecilia's graduate and a student at Roman Catholic, he knows how to have a good time, being a good time himself.

"Ey you got the jawns?"

Donny looks over at The Kid, asking him if he's got the stuff. The Kid peers around suspiciously, making sure no one's watching them. He reaches into his bag and pulls out a pack of Newports and tosses them to Donny.

No one really knows his name, so everyone just calls him The Kid. He's pretty much the go-to guy for us whenever we need something around Fox Chase. Cigs. Alc.

Nic. You name it, he can get it for you. He's got a trimmed beard and a mop of hair that makes him look like he's thirty, but he's probably only a senior at Northeast High.

    Probably.

    Donny stares down at the teal-green color of the box, the thick gold line that's tattooed into his brain like a bad dream.

    Donny pops open the box and sticks the little white stick into his mouth and lights it, feeling the potent taste of tobacco hit his mouth and engulf in his lungs like a wildfire. He breathes out, sitting under the cool autumn sun as the wind blows through his hair and smoke as he takes another drag from his cigarette, losing track of time.

    "DONNY, YOU'RE UP NEXT!"

    Shea's scream echoes loudly, seemingly heard from the tracks. Donny flicks the cigarette butt away from the bench and runs up to the backstop, grabbing the yellow bat with electrical tape wrapped tightly around the handle, and steps up to the plate.

"EASY OUT!"

Donny grips the bat, releasing anger through his white knuckles, now glued to the electrical tape grip on the bat. He watches intently as the white plastic whistles through the air and he whiffs.

0-1.

He shakes his head and brushes it off. He steps forward, taps the corners of the dish and gets into his stance. He swings. . .

0-2.

He steps up to the plate and takes a deep breath, letting his grip loosen on the bat as he stares down the pitcher, who's smirking at him from the mound. He smiles as the pitcher steps back for the pitch. He winds up and throws it, the ball whistling through the air with blistering speed, only to be hit square and sent flying through the air.

"RUN DONNY! RUUUUUN!"

Donny breaks into a dead sprint as he watches the left fielder turn around and keep running, turning into a blip as Donny rounds the bases.

"DIG! DIG! DIG!"

His teammates, who are yelling at him from the outside of the fence, wave him home. Donny's sprint picks up ever so slightly, feeling his ankles scream at his brain in agony as the cleats are throwing dirt behind him with every step. Approaching the plate, the white plastic whistle is heard over Donny's ear.

"SLIDE!"

The ball drops from the air over Donny's shoulder into the catcher's hands as Donny lunges off his back foot, throwing his entire one-seventy body weight forward, slamming into the catcher with incomprehensible force. The catcher flies back as Donny's weight drops onto the plate. The whole field stands silent as they watch the hands of the catcher, the guardian of home plate, lose grip and drop the bright white plastic ball into the dirt.

"SAFE!"

The benches erupt with an onomatopoeia of boos, curses and cheers as Donny jumps to his feet, punching the air and high-fiving his teammates.

"Now that was awesome."

"Ey thanks Shea."

Donny and Shea dab each other as the rest of the day flies by. Just as the sun begins to set, the game ends, with Donny's team winning eleven to ten, with Donny's homer giving them the lead near the end. The group of kids part their ways as Donny and Patty leave the beautiful Daniel Sweeney ballfield.

"That was a good game. I think I cawled it pretty fair."

"Yeah, you cawled a great game Patty . . ."

Donny pauses and takes a swig of water, feeling the rush of the cool liquid flush down his throat.

"Except for that cawl you made durin the beginnin."

"Are you still pissed off bout that?"

"Yeah, I'm pissed off bout it. It was three feet off the plate!"

"Donny. Baby. You can't see it the way I see it. It clipped the corner. Swear to Go-"

"Bullshit! Clipped the corner my ass . . ."

The two boys fought and bickered and talked about the game as they walked down Rhawn Street towards Oxford as the sun set more and more in the far off yet seemingly close distance.

"You wanna make a quick stop at Wawa real quick?"

"Sure. I'm always hungry. Might get some wooder too. I'm really thirsty."

Wawa is approximately the greatest chain of convenience stores in the nation, known for their good food, amazing hoagies and delicious coffee.

And I mean delicious cawfee.

The two boys walk down the tracks near Fox Chase Station and cut through the hole in the fence to get into the Wawa parking lot. They get some food and drinks and start walking back to Rhawn and Verree.

"Ey, I need to stop at Keller's. I need to get lunch meat for dinner tonight."

"Aight. See ya later Donny."

The two boys part their ways as Donny walks into the little mom and pop store and after getting the food, walks home, watching the bright sun set more and more, turning the sky a blood orange hue.

    Today was perfect.

III

 The noise of an alarm clock slaps Donny across his face like a knockout punch. He springs up from his slumber, looking around his room, painted green and white. A die-hard Birds fan and a Phils fan since birth. He rolls out of bed and shuffles downstairs, feeling his socks slide against the rough carpet of the steps.

 "Mornin Donny."

 "Mornin Ma."

Donny walks over to the kitchen cabinet and grabs some cereal, pouring it into a bowl and tearing into it like a ravenous dog, the milk and cereal splashing as he brings the spoon from the bowl to his mouth with rapid speed.

"Hey, is your brother awake yet? You need to get'im up. He's got a meet at nine."

Donny sighs, puts the spoon down and walks upstairs, walking down the hallway.

"WAKE UP! LET'S GO!"

Donny kicks the bedroom door in and walks over to the bunk bed, shaking it harshly, hearing the wood creak louder and louder with every tug.

"Oh come on, Donny, can't you wait a little longer? I'm tryin to sleep up'ere!"

"No sleep. You got a meet at nine. You need to go."

Dom shoots his body up like rising from the grave.

"Aw . . . I forgot bout that."

Dominic Issac Mooney is Donny's older brother, a year older than him and kinda the jokester of the family. Dom is Donny's right hand man in the family. If Donny's got something on his chest and knows he can't go to anyone about it, Dom's always there to help him. The two have formed an inseparable bond amongst each other, helping each other out, especially with the illegal stuff.

Dom races downstairs, book bag in hand as he grabs a granola bar before heading out of the door.

"See ya Ma!"

"See-"

The door slams shut as Dom races down the sidewalk and hops in his car.

"-Ya."

Donny stumbles down the steps and sits in the living room, watching TV as he devours his cereal. The sound of light footsteps creaking down the stairs hits Donny's ears like a bad memory.

"Wassup Loser."

"Wassup Idiot."

Felicity Noreen Mooney, or just Lissy, is Donny's sister, a year younger than him. Their relationship is . . . complicated, as their idea of being siblings involves them just insulting each other twenty-four seven. It's just their way of showing each other love. But still, that's a weird way of showing it.

All three kids were 'Irish triplets', as his mother had Dom, then him, then Lissy all around ten to eleven months apart. How the hell you do that, Donny had no clue, but regardless, after Lissy, his mom was *done* with kids after that.

Lissy walks into the kitchen, gets a bowl of cereal and walks into the living room. She walks past Donny and snatches the remote as she walks past him.

"Yo, I was watchin somthin."

"Well, I'm watchin somthin now."

Lissy flips the channel from Donny's show to hers. Donny drops his spoon into his bowl, fuming mad.

"Listen, I had the remote first, I get to watch what I wanna watch. You can watch somthin after I'm done"

Lissy smirks at Donny, transferring her gaze right back to the TV set. Donny reaches over and yanks the remote from his sister's tight grasp.

"MOOOOOM!"

"WHAT?"

A scream conversation between his sister and mother ensues as he sits down to watch his show.

"DONNY TOOK THE REMOTE FROM ME!"

"DONNY, GIVE THE REMOTE BACK TO YOUR SISTER!"

"BUT LISSY TOOK IT FROM ME FIR-"

"I DON'T WANNA ARGUE WIT YOU. GIVE IT!"

Donny sighs annoyed as he rolls his eyes and chucks the remote at his sister.

"It's only cause you're the baby of the family."

Lissy smirks at Donny and flagrantly puts her show on. Donny rolls his eyes and goes onto his phone. He scrolls aimlessly through social media as a text notification pops up.

'Yo, you free rn?'

It's a text from his friend Shane.

'Yeah, should be. Just eating breakfast.'

Donny looks up from his phone and looks at the show Lissy is watching.

"Why do you watch this? It's such a dumbass show."

"WATCH YOUR MOUTH DONNY!"

Donny rolls his eyes as he feels his phone vibrate in his hand.

'Cool. Wanna play ball later?'

'Sure, just us two or a group?'

Donny looks over at Lissy and rolls his eyes. *Such a dumbass show.*

Bzzz bzzz.

'Just us two. I was texting people but no one was answering.'

'Aight. I'll be out soon.'

Donny finishes the last slurps of his cereal-y milk and runs into the kitchen.

"Hey Ma. Shane asked if I could hang out today. Is that okay?"

"Yeah, once you finish doin your stuff, you can go."

Donny thanks his mom and runs upstairs, grabbing his bag and races downstairs. He quickly straightens up the living room, vacuums and races out of the door. As soon as he gets out of the house, his hurried sprint turns to a screeching halt.

"Aw damn it, Dom took the car."

Donny hops on his phone and texts Dom.

'Yo, what time's the meet over?'

Donny looks up at the sky, clearer and bluer than anything he's ever seen.

'Should be over by 11. Why?'

'Hangin out today and I need the car.'

Donny looks up from his phone as he sees a car drive down his street and park in front of the house to the right of him.

"How's it goin, Donny boy?"

He waves at the man driving his big gray pickup truck.

"Goin good, Mr. Rob."

Bzzz bzzz.

'Aight. You can have it when I'm back.'

Donny looks down and texts Shane.

'I'll be over in a little. Dom's got the car right now.'

Mr. Rob is walking up his path, carrying a big bag of groceries.

"How's school goin?"

"Eh, it's goin okay. Still got a year left. Kinda sucks."

Mr. Rob nods his head as he opens the gate to a fenced area on the side of the house.

"How's Dom doin?"

"He's doin good."

Donny looks down at his phone, peering to see if Shane responded yet.

"Does Dom know where he's goin to college yet?"

"Yeah, I think he's goin to Temple."

"Good for him. Smart kid."

Bzzz bzzz.

'Aight. Let me know when you're on your way over.'

Donny puts down his phone and goes inside his house. He sits down on the couch and continues playing on his phone when suddenly, he hears a 'whoosh' in the air and the TV remote crashes right in his forehead. He looks up, eyes squinted from the pain, to see Lissy walking away from him into the kitchen.

"You can watch your show now, Loser."

"WHAT THE FUC-"

"DONALD RICHARD MOONEY!"

Donny grumbles from his mother's cry.

"Hey Lissy . . ."

She turns around mid-walk and peers at her brother, hand pressed against his head in pain.

"You're fuckin dead."

Donny drops the remote and bolts into the dining room, chasing his sister around the table.

"DONNY! STOP!"

Donny's racing back and forth around the table, finally catching up to her and pulling her to the floor. He gets on top of her and holds her arms down. He inhales nasally, feeling the spit and saliva roll down his throat and onto his tongue, forming the biggest loogie ever as he hears a car pull up in front of the house.

"I'll get you next time, Loser."

He slurps loudly, pulling the mucus back into his throat and swallows it down, grabbing his phone and book bag and heads out the door. He opens the door and runs past Dom, who's holding the keys out for him.

"Thanks bro."

"Ey, you might need to fill'er up. I think she's pretty low."

Donny hops into the car and turns the key, listening to the engine turn over and the gauges light up. He puts it in drive and pulls away, watching his house become smaller and smaller in the side-view mirrors. He turns off of Verree and onto Rhawn. He turns on his phone and dials up Shane.

'Hey Shane.'

'Yo wassup?'

'I'm on my way. I'll be there in a few.'

'Aight. See ya then.'

Shane hangs up as Donny cruises down Rhawn Street, past the Rite Aid, past Datillo's and past Checkers. He turns onto the Boulevard and pushes down on the gas, feeling the rumble of the engine as he watches the speedometer tick move.

Twenty.

Thirty.

Forty.

Fifty.

Donny's flying down the Boulevard in his little old black sedan as he rolls to a stop at Grant and the Boulevard. He looks around and turns onto Grant, only to be cut off by some asshole in a truck. Donny watches as the bearded middle-aged man curses him out through the windshield. Donny gives him a swift finger and gases it down Grant.

He pops a window open as he cruises down the road, smiling in the midday sun, looking at the neon signs that cover Nifty Fifty's, shining so brightly you could see them from the top of the Comcast Center.

Donny looks down and sees the tank is almost empty. He flicks on his turn signal and pulls into Wawa, whipping around and pulling up next to the pump. After filling up his tank, he pulls away from the pump and into a parking spot. He taps MAC, grabs a soda and hops back into the car, starting it up and driving down Grant. He turns onto Academy and watches the planes fly in and out of Northeast Airport. As he passes Chalfont, he rolls back the sunroof on top of his car.

"FUCK RYAN!"

Donny sticks his hand out of the sunroof and sticks the middle finger at the inanimate building, driving past Archbishop Ryan High School as he flies down Academy, the bystanders looking at the black car in confusion. Being a Judge boy, Donny felt it in his blood to do this.

The legendary Northeast Catholic high school rivalry. Ryan versus Judge. To call this a rivalry is an understatement to say the least. This rivalry includes hatred towards any and all persons who attend the opposing school. This rivalry has led to fights, suspensions, expulsions, you name it, it's happened because of this rivalry. Nevertheless, it's infused in the blood and hearts of the students of these schools and my God, do they embrace it.

He pulls his hand back into the car and rolls the sunroof closed. He drives past St. Martha's and pulls onto Comly, slowing down as he pulls over to the side of the road, in front of Shane's house. Donny honks the horn several times, just as he sees a door open from the nerve-ending sight of row homes, as Shane races down his sidewalk, basketball in hand and hops in the car.

"Wassup Shane."

Donny and Shane dab each other up as Donny pulls into the road and slowly drives down Comly.

Shane Douglas Murphy. Donny met Shane at Judge's open house and the two have kept in contact since. They've grown to be good friends at Judge and play baseball together at Judge, as well as for a few rec leagues. If they both keep improving, they think they'll both make captains. It's going to be a good year.

"Whatchu in the mood to do?"

Shane looks up from his phone, puts his backpack down and peers out of the window, thinking of something to do.

"I dunno Donny. Let's go to Palmer and play some ball for now."

"Aight. I'm down."

Donny whips a u-bee at the end of the street and drives back up Comly, pulling into the playground.

"I got some stuff for us to have fun."

Donny parks the car and hops out, the sound of his slides scraping the asphalt in the parking lot. Shane grabs his book bag and basketball and jogs to the courts. Donny watches as a group of girls walks across the playground from the parking lot, but he only knows one of them. Erin. She looks at Donny and sees him looking at her and she smiles and waves, Donny feeling his cheeks become red and his heart beat fast.

"Donny, the fuck you doin? Let's go!"

He jumps from his friend's shout and jogs towards the courts.

"Pass it."

Shane dribbles and passes the ball to Donny, who jumps up and drains a three.

"Nice shot."

Donny grabs the ball and passes it to Shane, who drives it in, laying it up to the basket.

"Gimme a min."

Donny watches as Shane jogs over to his book bag. Donny takes a couple shots in his absence, sinking a few and missing others.

"Here. Catch."

Donny hears a 'whoosh' and turns his head, watching a metallic flash in the sunlight, reaching out and grabbing the object, feeling the cool metal rush against his palm.

"I have a couple more in my book bag if you're feelin it."

Donny looks down and smiles at the beer can, the silver can with blue and red smiling right back. Donny cracks open the can, hearing the satisfying sizzle against his ear.

ckCRKtsh sssssshhhhhh

Donny burps and puts down the can, dribbling the ball and running towards the net, jumping and laying it into the basket.

"So who was the chick, Donny?"

Donny looks over at his friend, who's now chugging a can of Natty and shooting the ball.

Glp glp glp

Ahhhhhh

"Erin."

Erin Kaylee White, is Donny's grade-school crush. Donny knows her from Cecilia's, as they both graduate the same year. Donny's been dying to ask her out but hasn't worked up the courage to do it.

Donny bounces the ball and shoots it, watching it as it hits rim and bounces towards Shane.

"The girl you've had a crush on since like fourth grade?"

Donny peers at his friend, who's giving him a smirk with a look.

"Yep."

Donny blushes as he shoots and misses, watching the ball hit off the backboard and bounce down the court.

"Did'ya tawk to'er?"

Shane jumps up and drains a three from thirty feet back.

"Whooo! I'm on fire!"

Donny laughs at his friend, grabbing the ball as it bounces towards him.

"Nah. I haven't tawked to'er much."

"Dude, you went to the same school. You don't have'er Snap or somethin like that."

"I dunno man."

Donny bounces it and shoots, completely airballing it into the fence behind the hoop.

"Aight. somethin's off here Donny."

"Whatchu mean 'somethin's off'?"

Shane stares at his friend in disbelief.

"You just missed three shots in a row. You never do this bad."

Donny nods his head and agrees with friend.

"Just too scared to tawk to'er bro. Besides, I don't need that kinda worry in my life right now."

Donny dribbles that ball and passes it to Shane.

"Aight. I get it. Calm down."

Donny sits down on the fence and tops off his beer.

Glp glp glp

Ahhhhhh

Donny crushes the can under his slides, his face suddenly breaking into a smirk.

"Ey Shane?"

Donny peers over at Shane, who's chugging his second can, topping it off and burping loudly, chucking the can into the trash can.

"Yeo?"

"One on one?"

Shane smiles wildly, tying his shoelaces and hops to his feet.

"You're on!"

Donny hops to his feet and races over to Shane's book bag, grabbing a can.

"Gotta make it even for you."

Shane peers at Donny and shakes his head, smirking and smiling at him as he cracks it open and chugs it down.

Donny crushes it against his head and tosses it into the trash, Shane looking at the red marks from the can on Donny's temple as Donny bounces around the court, the rush of beer giving him a sudden jolt of energy.

"You know the rules Shea. Let's go."

"Check."

Shane bounces the ball towards him.

"What we playin too?"

Donny catches the ball and jumps, draining a three on his first shot of the game.

"Till we're bored."

The two boys play their hearts out for hours as the day slowly goes by. Donny and Shane play the score up higher and higher, slowly losing count as the sun sets, eventually blocked out by Flyers Skate Zone. The red-violet color stretches across the sky like a portentous painting. Sweaty and tired, the two boys walk back to the parking lot and sit on the car hood.

"That was wild, Donny."

"It was. Too bad ya lost."

Donny smirks at Shane, who scoffs in his face.

"No shot I lost. I beat you."

Donny reaches into Shane's bag and grabs another beer.

"Till it got too dark, I was drainin three after three."

Donny reaches back into the bag and hands Shane the last beer.

"Yea but you couldn't stop me in the paint, Donny."

"Let's just settle it at a draw and we'll get back to this later?"

"Agreed."

The two boys top off their beers, toss the cans away and hop in the car to drive home.

Today was fantastic.

IV

Donny wakes up to the sound of his mother in the shower and his siblings walking through the hallway and down the stairs.

"DONNY! TIME FOR MASS! WAKE UP!"

Donny sighs loudly and rolls out of bed, his hair strewn aimlessly about his head. He walks down the hallway, just as his Mom is leaving the bathroom.

"Mornin Donny."

"Ugh."

Lissy walks up the stairs and cackles at her brother.

"Nice hair dumbass."

"Lissy . . ."

Donny's mom peers at his sister, who rolls her eyes and peers down at her phone.

"Really? I say that and I get screamed at but she says it and all she gets is a look?"

His mom peers right back at Donny, who rolls his eyes and walks into the bathroom.

"Don't gimme the attitude right now, Donny. I'm not in the mood."

Donny slams the bathroom door shut and rolls his eyes, speaking silently to himself.

He shakes his head clear of the anger and hops in the shower, feeling his body wash away of all the anger and everything that's making him pissed off and upset. He hops out and cleans himself up, looking fairly decent. He puts on his Eagles sweatshirt, his black joggers and his hightop Vans. He brushes his hair back and sits on the couch downstairs.

Bzzz bzzz.

Donny takes his phone out of his pocket to look at the text.

'*Hey Donny. A couple of people are hangin later at my house, do you wanna come?*'

'*Yeah. I'm down. What time later?*'

He stares at his phone, waiting for a response, the noise of his household turning into white noise as he focuses his mind on the texts.

'*Probably around like 5 at my house.*'

'*Yeah, my folks'll be fine wit it.*'

Donny put his phone back in his pocket, just as his family is leaving the house for church.

"Come on, Donny. Time to go."

The Mooney family drives to St. Cecilia's, pulling into the parking lot and going through the motions of Mass. They get out of the church and get to the car.

"Hey Ma, Aidan asked if I wanted to hang wit'im today. Is that okay?"

His father looks at his mother, who sighs slowly.

"Yea. That's okay Donny. Who else is gonna be there?"

Donny pulls out his phone, thinks for a moment and reads the text.

"Me, Aidan, Paul, Benny, Ricky, Jimmy, Rose, Lisa and Bridget."

His father peers even harder at his mom, who sighs more quickly.

"Who're the girls?"

Donny peers at his dad, who stares straight forward.

"Rose, Lisa and Bridget? They're Benny's, Ricky's and Paul's girlfriends. They're fun girls. They're not troub-"

"What time will you be home?"

Donny's dad interjects, cutting him off.

"I dunno. Eleven?"

His father turns around and looks at Donny dead in the eyes.

"It's a school night."

Donny rolls his eyes and interjects his dad's statement.

"I finished my homework. I'll be home at eleven. Is that fine Ma?"

Donny's dad turns back around as his mother slowly nods. Mr. Mooney starts the car and drives home, parking the car in front of his house upon arrival. Donny walks inside and then upstairs to get changed and grab his keys.

"Wassup Loser."

Dom walks in and sits down on the bottom bunk, playing on his phone in the process.

"Sup Loser."

Donny opens his dresser and rummages through it, looking for his wallet and keys, to no avail.

"Hey Dom?"

Donny peers over at his brother, who's munching on a protein bar, mouth full of food.

"Yeo?"

"You know where my keys are?"

Dom looks at his brother and crunches down on the bar, with speckles of it dribbling off of his lips and from the corner of his mouth.

"If it was up your ass, you'd know where it was."

Donny rolls his eyes and chuckles at his brother's comment.

"I think they're in my bureau."

Dom gets up and pops opens his drawer, grabbing the keys and tossing them to Donny.

"Did'ya fill'er up last time?"

Donny catches the keys and is mid-way out the door before his brother asks him the question.

"Uhh yea. Filled'er up on my way to Shane's."

"Good. You know how Mom doesn't like it when we go out wit an empty tank."

"Yeah. I know."

Donny nods his head and walks out of his bedroom.

"See ya Loser."

Dom's shout from his room makes Donny smirk as he walks downstairs and out of the door.

"See ya Ma. See ya Dad."

"Stay safe!"

Donny slams the door shut as he walks down the sidewalk and hops in his car. He puts the car in drive, hearing the engine rumble as he plugs his phone into the speakers. He's scrolling through his music as he stops on a song, starts it up and drives away from his house. *I don't really care if you cry.* Donny pulls off of Rhawn and turns onto Verree, cruising down the street, bumping to the music. *Phantom that's all red.* He looks at his phone as he stops at the light next to Baldi. His phone starts ringing and he answers it as the light turns green.

'*YEO! WASSUP DONNY!*'

Donny pulls the phone away from his head, his friend's booming voice assaulting his ear.

'*Yeo wassup!*'

'*Nuthin much. Paul and Ricky showed up. You on the way?*'

Donny looks at his phone.

'Yea, I'm about fifteen, twenty minutes out.'

'Aight bet. See ya soon.'

Donny hangs up the phone and turns off Verree and onto Alburger, driving until he gets to Krewstown. He pulls into Wawa and grabs some grub before heading to Aidan's house. He hops in the car and takes a deep breath. After a few minutes of contemplation, he reaches into his pocket and pulls out his phone. He scrolls through his numbers, eventually finding the right one. Slowly, he clicks on it, dialing the number.

Boooooooooot.

Booooooooot.

'Hello?'

Donny's face turns beet red. He takes a deep breath and exhales loudly.

'Hello?'

'Hey Erin.'

'Hey Donny, how's it going?'

Donny's mind is going a million miles a minute, coming up short of words to say to her.

'Nuthin much . . .'

An awkward silence ensues between the two teens.

'Hey, are you free right now? If you aren't, I completely understa-'

'No, I'm free. My folks aren't home. Looking for an excuse to leave.'

Donny feels his heart beating out of his chest.

'Cool, I'm hangin out wit a buncha my friends. You wanna join me?'

Donny hears her giggles through the phone speakers. It makes his heart giddy.

'Hell yeah. I'm down. Where are you guys meeting?'

Donny thinks, his mind running blank but then it comes back to him.

'I'm just heading to my friends house on Morefield now. I'll swing by and pick you up?'

Her giggle becomes louder and more obvious.

'Sure. I live on Banes. Right off of Welsh.'

'Perfect. I'm at the Wawa at Krewstown, I'll be there in a few.'

'See you then.'

The dial tone hits Donny's ear and he ends the call. He lays back in the car seat and sighs loudly, a smile slowly stretching across his face.

You fuckin did it Donny.

He puts the car in drive and pulls out of the Wawa parking lot, driving down Grant. He merges onto Welsh and looks for Banes, finding it and pulling onto the street. He slows down and stops at the end of the block, looking for her address. He hears a screen door close shut and the clack of shoes moving down the sidewalk.

"Hey!"

A tap on the passenger door catches Donny off guard as he pops the lock and Erin hops in.

She looks fuckin beautiful.

"Hey Erin."

The way her name sounds is gorgeous.

"So, you ready?"

"I'm ready if you are."

She smiles at him as he puts the car in drive.

Her smile is perfect.

He whips a u-bee and drives down Welsh to Grant, pulling onto Krewstown. He drives past Bustleton Swim Club, the pool emptied of its water, closed for the season. He drives down Krewstown until he turns onto Morefield, pulling up to his friend's house. He walks up to the door and knocks, his mother answering the door.

"Hey Mrs. Smith. Is Aidan here?"

Mrs. Smith smiles at Donny and Erin.

"He is. One moment. AIDAN!"

She pauses for a moment, waiting for an answer.

"AIDAN!"

"I'M BUSY MA!"

She sighs loudly before inhaling sharply.

"AIDAN DANIEL, GET YOUR ASS UP'ERE RIGHT NOW. DONNY'S HERE!"

Mrs. Smith's yell is followed by loud, thundering footsteps from the basement stairs.

"Aye! Donny!"

Aidan walks over to Donny and dabs him up. He looks at the girl next to him and constraints his gape.

"Oh, Erin, this is Aidan."

She looks up at Aidan, an immense teenager, standing at six foot four and waves at him shyly. Aidan claps his hands and directs the two teens down to the basement, stopping Donny as Erin walks down the stairs.

"Oh my God, you actually did it Donny."

"I know I did it. No need to be surprised."

Aidan chuckled at Donny and both boys go downstairs. Donny walks down the basement steps to a group full of girls and boys, who all greet him spectacularly.

"DONNY!"

He chuckles at their cheers and walks around the room, dabbing his friends up and hugging the girls before sitting on the couch.

"Hey Erin!"

"Hey Bridget!"

Erin walks over and the two girls hug for a few seconds before Bridget turns around, sitting next to Benny and Erin sitting next to Donny.

"Everyone, this is Erin."

"Hey guys."

The group waves and smiles at the girl, a few of the boys throwing winks at Donny.

"Erin, this is Paulie, Lisa, Rose and as you know, Benny and Bridget"

Erin waves again at everyone. Donny leans back on the couch and looks over at Aidan.

"Where's Jimmy?"

Aidan takes a gulp of his soda and puts the can down on the table.

"He's at Lucky Sevens. He should be back soon."

Donny nods his head and looks over at his friends.

"Paulie, Lisa, how youse guys been doin?"

Paulie throws his arm around Lisa's shoulder and pulls her closer into him.

Paul Joseph Caruso, Paulie to everyone (or "Guido" if you wanna piss him off). A graduate of Christ the King and student at Archbishop Ryan, he is probably the most Italian kid in the Northeast. A lean, tall kid, with a mop of thick, black hair and a neck beard that extends down to his chest. Knows how to cook, can speak the language fluently and knows how to rumble. Hell of a time. Hell of a kid.

Lisa Kaitlen Anderson. Grew up in the suburbs of Delco and moved here to Parkwood before kindergarten. A graduate of St. Anselm's and a student at Archbishop Ryan, she's a hardcore field hockey player and runs on her spare time. A lot of fun to be around.

"We're doin pretty good. It'll be what, three months in two weeks right?"

Lisa ponders for a second and nods at Donny.

"Yeah, November fifteenth'll be three months."

"Good for youse. How bout youse over there Benny?"

Bridget and Benny look up from their phones, seemingly clueless at Donny.

Bridget Rachael Sullivan. Grew up in Parkwood, a graduate of St. Martha's and a student at George Washington High School, she's Erin's best friend, since they met at school their freshman year. Great person to be around.

"Uhh . . . we've been good. It'll be what . . . eighteen months in December, right Bridge?"

Bridget shakes her head without peering away from her phone.

"Eighteen in January."

Donny smiles and nods at them.

"Good for youse."

They smile and nod their heads at him. Donny looks over and peers at Rose.

"Wassup Rose!"

Rose throws a peace sign at him and smiles.

Rose Patricia Jones. Graduate of Maternity BVM and a student of Archbishop Ryan, she's best friends and teammates with Lisa, both playing field hockey for Ryan and both on NHS. Smart girl and a hell of a time.

"Wassup Donny!"

"Nuthin much. How you been dealin?"

She leans back and stretches her body out on the couch.

"I'm dealin, ya know. Ricky's been pretty good to me so far."

Donny nods and smiles. He looks around the room, becomes confused and looks over at Aidan.

"Speakin of which, where is Ricky?"

The basement becomes silent as everyone looks around and shrugs, only to have the sound of a flushing toilet to cut through the silence. A door opens as Ricky stumbles out of the bathroom, whips out a pen and rips it, holding in the vapor, coughing subtly as he exhales it. He looks over at Donny, his eyes more red than a Phils hat.

"Yeo Donny!"

He stumbles over to Donny and dabs him up.

Ricardo Thomas Garcia, or Ricky, is a wild child to say the least. Half Puerto Rican, Half Irish, he's a fun time to be around. His hobbies include binge-drinking at kegs and hot-boxing the bathrooms with his dab pen. A Resurrection Parish graduate, Archbishop Ryan student and heavy weed smoker, he's a great guy to be around, sober or not.

"Wassup Ricky. You good?"

Ricky nods his head, swaying back and forth like a tree in the wind.

"Ya know, I'm doin quite fine, Donald."

He giggles at himself and peers over at Erin and his mouth gapes.

Donny's face turns an embarrassed red color as he turns towards Erin.

"Um. . .Ricky, this is Er-"

"Erin! Ya did it Donny!"

Ricky dabs him up and turns around to the group, sitting on the floor in front of Rose, smiling like a madman at Donny. The front door opening and closing upstairs can be heard

from the basement, followed by footsteps down the stairs.

"JIMMY!"

The group shouts at Jimmy as he comes down the stairs, his book bag stretched to the max

James Arnold Hansen, better known as Jimmy. Jimmy is Donny's right-hand guy when it comes to getting stuff for him. Two years older than him, Jimmy is a graduate of St. Cecilia's, alumni of Father Judge, a student at Temple University and German-bred like a fucking dog. Hell of a kid.

"AY! Wassup everybody."

Jimmy dabs everyone up and stops at Erin.

"Who's this?"

Donny's face turns red and he chokes on his words.

"Jimmy, this is Erin."

Jimmy nods his head towards her, turning around and sitting down next to Aidan.

"So, what's the plan?"

Aidan looks around the room to everyone shrugging and shaking their heads.

"If youse are down, we could go to the skate zone and then hang here after?"

He looks around the room, everyone nodding their heads in agreement.

"Aight cool. We'll head out now."

The group nod their heads and stand up, moving out of the basement one by one. They all leave and get to their cars. Donny holds the door open for Erin as she gets in the car. He hops in and starts the car, typing in the address to the skate zone.

"So where is the skate zone?"

Donny looks away from his phone and furrows his brow for a second.

"It's right near Ryan. A little down Comly."

Erin nods her head and faces forward as Donny gets the car rolling down the street. He looks at her as she's looking at her phone.

She's beautiful.

"So, uh . . . you ever been skatin before?"

She smiles briefly and shakes her head.

"Me neither."

Donny drives back down Krewstown and turns onto Grant, cruising down the street, crossing over the Boulevard, passing Millers and Whitman Square Shopping

Center. They turn onto Academy and cruise down the street, turning onto Comly and pulling into the parking lot. He parks the car and gets out with Erin in tow. They get inside and it's packed. The group gets out of the cold autumn night and inside the building, noise battering throughout the walls of the skate zone. After ten minutes, they finally get to the register.

"2 people."

A teenage girl, who's working the register, types on it aimlessly without expression.

"Skates included?"

"Uh. . . yea."

After a few seconds of clacking on the register, she looks up with a blank face.

"That'll be thirty total."

Donny and Erin both take out their wallets.

"No, I got this."

He takes out a twenty and a ten, handing to the girl in exchange for two stickers.

The two teens walk over to the skate rental and wait in the back of the line.

"Hey Donny . . ."

Donny looks at Erin and tries his hardest not to smile like a fool.

"Yeo?"

"I can pay for my half."

Donny looks at her wallet, still in her hand, looks up and smiles at her.

"I know."

They get to the front of the line and wait for the male teen to walk from the wall of skates to the counter.

"What can I getchu, boss?"

"Nine and a half."

The teen moves his finger from Donny to Erin.

"And you, miss?"

"Uh seven and a half please."

He taps the counter and walks to the racks on racks of skates, Erin staring at the walls covered floor to ceiling.

"Nine and a half annnnnnnnd seven and a half."

The two teens thank the man and sit down at the tables, putting on their skates.

"What did your friends mean when they said 'ya did it'?"

Donny gulps empty air and blushes.

"I'll tell you later. I promise."

Erin peers at Donny mysteriously and shrugs as the rest of the group comes over and joins them.

"Come on guys. Let's go!"

Bridget and Benny stand up and step over to the rink, hopping onto the ice. The group eventually follow the couple, with Donny and Erin in the back.

"You got good balance?"

Donny looks over at Erin and shakes his head.

"Nope. I got horrible balance."

The two teens stumble onto the ice. Donny manages to stay upright and glide away from the wall, while Erin stays on the wall, hands glued to it. He goes slowly, keeping her company as the group of teens split apart, some flying around the ring and some taking it slow.

"Come on, Erin, just take a step away from the wall."

She takes a deep breath, gaining confidence and pushes off the wall, colliding into Donny. He catches the brunt of the force and stays upright. Donny looks over at her and smiles.

"See, that wasn't that hard."

Erin looks up at Donny and smiles, making his heart beat out of his chest and warms his body in the freezing climate of the ice rink. The two walk around the rink, just cruising next to each other, both blushing but neither saying a word. Ricky flies past the two and slides to a stop.

"Ay, it's almost eight. We're gonna get outta here."

Donny looks over at Erin, smiles and looks back up at Ricky.

"Nah, we're good."

Ricky looks perplexed but nods his head after a second.

"You sure? Jimmy went to Lucky Sevens."

Donny shakes his head and politely declines.

"Some other night definitely. See ya Ricky!"

He throws up a peace sign and glides away on the skates. The two teens glide back off the rink and to the benches. They take their skates off and return them, walking back to the car. They both hop in and Donny shuts the door and plugs in his phone. He looks over at Erin, who's looking down at her phone.

"Ey Erin, you want to play somethin?"

She looks up from her phone to see Donny holding out his phone for her. She smiles vividly and takes his phone, scrolling through his songs.

"This is my song."

She taps on the song and it starts playing through the speakers. *I don't know what's next.*

"Woah. You an Uzi fan?"

She nods slowly as her body moves to the beat of the music. Donny looks over at her, her eyes closed and her body swaying with a smile across her face. Donny starts the car and looks out the window, hiding his vibrant smile from her. *I could never stress.* He drives forward and out of the parking lot. They're driving down Decatur and Donny looks over at Erin, who's still vibing with the music. *If you got hurt, yeah, I got hurt, yeah, I got bruised, too.*

"You hungry?"

Erin opens her eyes and looks up at Donny, smiling.

"Yeah, I'm hungry."

"Cool, I got a great place."

Donny pulls onto Comly and drives down the street, slowing down as they approach the Boulevard and pull into the parking lot of the Prince of Steaks.

Steve's.

They should call him the King of Steaks.

The sign brightly lit, showcasing majestic illumination of deliciousness. The two teens hop out of the car and walk inside, the place surprisingly filled for a school night. They walk up to the line, waiting in the back.

"You ever been here before?"

Erin moves her view from the menu to Donny.

87

"My dad took me to Pat's once but I've never been to Steve's."

Donny smiles and nods his head.

"In my opinion, Pat's and Gino's are tourist attractions. Jim's is second but Steve's takes the throne. Every time. All the time."

The two continue looking at the menu and advancing up the line, slowly approaching the register.

"What can I getchu fine people tonight?"

Donny nudges Erin in her arm, his face remaining fixed on the menu as he smiles.

"Could I get a cheesesteak, with onions and American please?"

The cashier nods and points his finger at Donny.

"Could I get a cheesesteak wit onions an whiz. A cheese fry annnd . . . Whatchu want?"

Erin looks at the drinks, pondering her choice of beverage.

"Pepsi."

"And two Pepsis."

The man clacks on the register for a few seconds, looking up after typing.

"Thirty, fifty-six is your total."

Erin pulls out her wallet and hands Donny a five.

"I got this."

She puts the five in his hand as he pulls out his wallet.

"Take the five."

He sighs and takes it from her, as he peers into his wallet.

Thank god.

He pays the man and the two teens sit down at the counter, waiting for their orders to be called.

"Hey Donny . . ."

Donny turns his head towards Erin and stifles a smile.

"Yeo?"

Erin turns her body, so she's facing Donny directly. Donny turns his body and does the same.

"Now that we're alone, what did your friends mean when they said 'ya did it'?"

Donny's face drains of all color except bright red. He looks down at his feet and then back up at Erin.

"Cause we went to the same school. Graduated the same year. Had a buncha classes together. And even though I go to Judge and you go to Washington, I can't seem to shake it."

Erin looks perplexed at Donny and moves her body towards him more.

"Can't shake what?"

Come on, Donny. Just say it!

"I've had a crush on you since fourth grade. I really wanted to ask you out on a date but never stomached the courage to do it."

Donny's body just slumps.

Holy shit. Ya did it kid.

His mind is at ease and his body feels like Jello. He looks up at her and she's looking at the ground. After a moment, she looks up at Donny with a smile.

"Well, I'm here. You finally did it. You got your date with me."

Both faces burst with joy, smiling from ear to ear.

"CHEESESTEAK WIT ONIONS AND AMERICAN, CHEESESTEAK WIT ONIONS AND WHIZ, CHEESE FRY AND TWO SODAS!"

Donny hops up from the chair and walks over to the pickup area, grabbing the food and bringing it over to the counter. The couple unwrap their steaks and pop open the styrofoam container holding the fries oozing with the cheesy liquid. The two lift their steaks and tap them together.

"Cheers!"

The couple immediately start plunging themselves into the steaks, enjoying the savory taste of steak, with cheesy onions dripping off the roll and onto the plate. They peer over at each other, mouths both full of cheesesteak goodness and smile. After a bit, they finish their steaks and consume the fries. They toss their trash and get to the car. As Donny opens the door for her, she sits down on the seat. As he's about to shut the door, she taps him on the back.

"Yeo?"

Donny turns around as she reaches out and pulls him in from his shirt, kissing him. Their amorous kiss lasts a few seconds as Donny closes his eyes, grateful for the night. She pulls away, the couple feeling like ecstasy. Donny stands up, still in a daze as to what just happened. He shuts the door and gets into the driver seat. He starts the car and plugs in his phone.

"Play whatever you want."

Donny hands his phone to her, smiling as he pulls out of the parking lot. He drives down the Boulevard, driving past Whitman Square and turns onto Grant. He drives down the street, turns onto Bustleton and then onto Banes, stopping in front of her house. He double-parks the car and gets out to walk her to her door. Erin turns around and faces Donny, smiling happily.

"Thank you so much for tonight, Donny."

Donny blushes from her words, smiling and looking at her like an idiot.

"Thank you too. Also, I was wonderin, if you aren't busy soon, if you were down for another date?"

Erin smiles at Donny and nods her head. Donny smiles and slowly walks backwards down the steps.

"Well, see ya soon."

Donny turns and walks down the steps, smiling and looking at his feet.

"Hey Erin . . ."

She turns around as Donny is right behind her, grabbing her face and pulling her in. The two kiss for what seems like forever. The two pull away from each other after a couple of minutes and they smile at each other.

"You're so beautiful."

"I love you Donny."

The two pull each other back together, kissing with the moon glowing in the night. This shit feels like a movie.

Today was fantastic.

V

Dom's alarm wakes him up as he rolls over in his bed to turn it off. Dom sits on his bed, rubs his eyes for a moment, contemplating his life. He stands up and bangs on the top bunk, waking Donny up.

". . . I'm up."

Donny looks over at his phone, the artificial light beaming into his eyes, searing them shut momentarily. The clock reads a quarter after six. He looks out the window, pitch black in the late weeks of November. The Monday before Thanksgiving day break.

Thank the Lord.

The two boys, eyes still closed from the early wake up call, walk around the room purely off of instinct. They brush their teeth, comb their hair, don their dress shirts, quarter zips and ties with the signature 'FJ' logo on it, walking down the stairs upon finishing. They see Lissy, who's racing around the kitchen, grabbing bread, peanut butter and jelly, making her sandwiches for school.

"Wassup Idiot."

Lissy continues making her sandwiches without even batting an eye at her brothers.

"Wassup Losers"

Lissy goes to Ryan, the natural-sworn enemy of Judge but Lissy got a full-ride there, so she's the exception to the case. Lissy, donned in her vibrant red polo and matte black skirt, Dom and Donny just standing there, watching Lissy race around the kitchen at the speed of sound for a few minutes, until Lissy is finished making her lunch. She grabs her bag, throws on a hoodie and opens the door, flipping her brothers off as the sound of the screeching screen door opening hits their ears.

"Peace out losers."

The door slams shut, echoing throughout the now deathly quiet household. Lissy races down Rising Sun and turns, near sprinting down Rhawn, barely catching the sixty-seven, now crowded with a tsunami of red and black. The two boys look at each other, perplexed.

"What's up wit'er?

Donny leans over to his brother and whispers into his ear

"I think it's that time of the month. . . ya know?"

Dom nods slowly and shrugs. Donny grabs a few slices of bread, slathers some PB and J on it and throws it into his bag. He opens the fridge, grabs a cup and pours a large cup of milk, putting the milk container away upon finishing. He lifts the cup up and chugs it down, drinking it all in a matter of seconds. After finishing it, he wipes the cloud white mustache off of his upper lip. The two boys grab their bags, lock the door and walk out of the house, hearing the echo of the slam from the inside hit their ears. They walk down their sidewalk, the chirp of the car unlocking beeps out loud as Dom pops the passenger door open, allowing Donny to sit down. He tosses his bland black Jansport book bag into the backseat of the car and goes onto his phone to talk to Erin.

'Hey.'

'Hey Donny.'

'How'd you sleep?'

'Good. Hbu?'

'Good. Watched a good movie last night.'

'Ouu! What movie . . .'

The couple talked endlessly as the boys rolled down Rhawn, cruising in the mid-dawn sun. After crossing over the creek, they turn onto Cresco, veer onto Rowland and then turn onto Solly. After parking the car, they walk towards the school, walking past the statue of St. Francis of DeSales and inside the school. Donny walks into the lunch hall and meets up with Benny and Aidan in the lunch hall. They all dab each other up and sit down at a table.

"So . . . How'd it go?"

"Ya know . . ."

Donny blushes and nods at his friends.

"Yeo!"

Benny and Aidan dab up Donny.

"Did'ya do it?"

Donny looks at his friends perplexed.

"Ya know . . ."

Ben imitates the explicit sexual act with his hands and Donny shakes his head while laughing.

"No. I didn't. Although . . . We're hangin again soon, so maybe next Saturday."

Benny and Aidan nod at him and they all chuckle at each other just as the clock hits five before eight. The bell rings and the boys get up and walk to their separate classrooms. They sit down as other Judge students file into the class. The onomatopoeia of the students batters the walls of school, the teacher talking to the boys, with the Crusader News Network playing in the background. The bell rings for the first period and the classes file out of their homerooms and to their first period classes. First up was biology. Donny hated biology. The teacher was an old lady who never taught a thing. Forty-five straight minutes of babbling. He must've fallen asleep in that class more times than he can count. The bell rings and he wakes up from his classroom slumber and rolls out of class, his eyes baggy and dark underneath them. He walks through the halls and passes Dom on the way to theology. Dom is walking with a group of guys, all who like Donny, except one. Branden Johnson.

Branden Keith Johnson. This dude was just an absolute dick to everyone, except for Dom but especially to Donny. He always shoved him in the hallways when Dom wasn't there. He called him all kinds of names you'd expect to hear as a freshman but not as an upperclassman. Unless you've committed social suicide, you were never bullied as an upperclassman. Regardless, once he entered that school, he was relentless. Non-stop torture. After freshman year, he seemed to lay off but he came back ten times worse this year, with talks of a fight between us but it never happened.

Theology was dumb. He went to Mass but his parents didn't really care, so he didn't care much either. He believes in God but doesn't really see himself as a religious person. The teacher didn't seem to care much either.

Though he didn't have lunch with either Benny or Aidan, he had third with Benny and fourth with Aidan. Donny loves two subjects, History and English. Third was History and they were learning about the American Revolution.

"Now gentlemen, what caused the American Revolution?"

. . .

The classroom silently sighs and looks around the room, waiting for someone to answer. A hand raises from the middle row.

"Mr. Mooney?"

"The graphs of y=f(x) and y=g(x) intersect in the first quadrant at the points (0, 2), (2, 4), and (A, B) = (1.032832, 2.401108)."

"Very good, Mr. Dominic."

Dom fist bumps one of his friends next to him as the class scribbles down the answer, the teacher writing it down on the board. Dom flips his AP Calculus notebook closed and puts it under his desk.

"Okay everyone, review over's. Time for the quiz."

"Yo Dom . . ."

Dom feels a tap and a whisper shoot over his ear.

"Wassup?"

Dom turns his head to look at Branden through his peripheral vision.

"I forgot to study. Can you help me?"

Dom turns his head a little more to look at Branden in the eyes.

"Dude. it's five questions. And it's all the shit we just studied."

"Just shut the fuck up and help me."

Dom rolls his eyes and nods his head.

"I gotchu. But I ain't helpin again. Just this one time."

As the teacher hands out the quiz paper, Dom reaches down for his notebook and quietly tears out a sheet of paper, hiding it under his leg. After the teacher passes Dom and Branden the paper, Dom gets to work.

"Okay gentlemen, you have ten minutes. Begin."

Since he studied, Dom easily finished the quiz in three minutes. Maybe two. It was a cake quiz for Dom. He takes out the piece of paper and places it on his desk. He quickly scribbles down the answers on the paper and folds it up.

"Pssst!"

Branden reaches for the page as the teacher is looking down at his computer. Branden immediately opens the page and starts writing down Dom's answers, flying through them, zoning out from his calculus scribble.

"Mr. Johnson . . ."

Branden looks up slowly, just finishing the final question.

"You won't be needing this anymore or this either."

The teacher grabs his quiz paper and his little answer key.

"GET YOUR ASS TO THE DEAN'S OFFICE!"

Branden grabs his bag and walks out of the room, expressionless. Dom is looking at the teacher, keeping his composure but sweating profusely. The teacher looks at the handwriting and recognizes it immediately. He looks up at Dom and lets out a heavy sigh. He looks at the cheat sheet again, crumbles it up and tosses it in the trash. Dom lets out a silent sigh and wipes his head of the sweat. Branden sits in the Dean's office, waiting for him to finish a phone call. He lays his head on his arms, closes his eyes and fades to sleep.

. . .

"Donny . . . Donny . . . MR. MOONEY! PLEASE WAKE UP!"

Donny's darkened eyes open to the painful sight of artificial classroom light. Benny and his History teacher, Mr. Hughes, were standing over him, looking at his fatigued body.

"Mr. Mooney, class is over. It's time for your next class."

Donny thinks for a second and realizes he has a Geometry test next period.

"Aw shit."

"Language, Mr. Mooney."

"Sorry, Mr. Hughes. Won't happen again."

Donny races out of class, races up the stairs and runs into his Geometry class.

"Mr. Donald. Nice of you to arrive. Don't worry about a late pass. I'll sort that out later."

The teacher hands him the test paper and it's all on lines. Perpendicular, parallel, stuff like that. Seems simple. It's not. He thought he liked geometry. Turns out it sucks. A lot. Donny's flipping through the test, seeing if he can pinpoint the easiest problem on the test. Having no luck, he flips to the front of the test and opens his calculator. He looks at the cover and realizes he has all of the formulas needed for the test. He props his cover behind his paper and plays around with his calculator. He places down his calculator and starts moving through the test quickly, looking up every few seconds to make sure the teacher isn't watching him.

"Twenty minutes left gentlemen. Twenty minutes left."

Donny starts panicking. He's through the first few questions but still has a considerable amount of the test left. He pulls out his cheat sheet and starts scribbling down the formulas, writing them at the top of the page. He starts working with the problems, some of them easier than he thought they would be. He hears his teacher walking up and down the rows of desks and students. He hears the taps of his dress shoes come closer and closer to him as he scribbles away on his test. The teacher arrives next to

Donny, who feels his presence over his right shoulder, just standing there, peering around the room. Sweating profusely, Donny reaches down to his bag and grab his water bottle, taking a long swig, feeling that sweet, sweet Philly lead water run down his throat, calming him down.

"Ahem."

Donny looks up at his teacher, who's staring at him with a look that could make hell freeze over.

"What's this?"

Really? This dude is gonna give me JUG for a fuckin wooder bottle?

"I'm sorry Mr. McCann. I'll put the wooder bottle away."

"Not the wooder bottle, Mr. Donald."

The teacher reaches down and grabs the calculator cover, showing Donny the formulas needed for the test.

"I'll see you after school. Right now, you have a trip to the Dean's office, Mr. Donald. I suggest you leave now before I get more upset."

Donny grabs his bag from off the floor and walks out of the classroom, walking to the Dean's office. He gets in there and sits down, waiting for the Dean to be finished with another student. He's sitting there, hearing the consistent, incessant sound of the Dean's assistant clacking away on her computer, probably doing something useless. The door opens as he hears the Dean say,

"Next time you're in here, it'll be for your expulsion!"

Branden walks out of the Dean's office, his face expressionless but beaming with anger. He looks over at Donny, becoming more angry by the sight of him.

"Next please."

Donny stands up and walks towards the office door as Branden is walking away.

"Wassup, little Mooney."

Donny eyeballs him briefly and as they pass, Donny sticks out his foot and trips him, turning his head to watch Branden stumble off his feet and face plant onto the red office carpet. He quickened his pace and walked into the office, shutting the door behind him, seeing Branden glaring at Donny like a bull at a matador. He turns around after closing the door and sits down in the hard, wooden chair, his bag dropping to his feet. Mr. Moore is a firm, built, middle-aged African-American man, with glasses and a neatly trimmed mustache.

"Mr. Mooney. What brings you here today?"

Donny's face goes red and he looks at Mr. Moore, dead in his eyes.

"I cheated on a math test."

Mr. Moore removes his glasses, rubs his eyes and brushes his mustache and chin, all the while looking at Donny with a look that could melt ice.

"Okay . . . Why did you do it?"

Donny sighs loudly and just shrugs his shoulders, looking at his feet.

"I didn't study and panicked. No excuses. One hundred percent my fault."

"Oh I know it is, Mr. Mooney."

Mr. Moore's booming voice caught Donny off guard and made him jump a little.

"You're the third student I've had to see students today cause of cheatin. I'm becomin sick and tired of all my students here 'not studyin' or even better 'forgettin to study'. You have your computers for a reason. Use them to your advantage. You have JUG for the next week. Get the fuck outta here."

Donny breathes in, grabs his bag and leaves the office, just as the bell is ringing. He makes his way to his accounting class, slowly catching his breath. The whole time the Dean was speaking, Donny didn't breathe, barely remembering anything he was saying. Except the JUG part. That part he heard clearly. He sits down in class and doesn't even feel anything during the class. Mentally, he flew through class. He walks to the lunch hall and sits down at a table with a bunch of kids he knows from classes but aren't really good friends with. He looks over his shoulder and sees his brother Dom across the room, who's sitting with all of his friends.

And Branden.

Branden looks around the lunch hall and sees Donny from across the room. He puts his food down, stands up and walks over to Donny, standing behind him as Donny is staring at his sandwich.

"Wassup faggot."

Donny takes a bite of his food, trying to ignore him.

"You listenin dickhead?"

Branden grabs Donny's shoulders and pulls him off the chair, sending him sprawling to the floor. Donny turns around, his body parallel to the ceiling, and sees Branden standing over him. He looks at Branden, his immense figure towering over Donny and tries to think quickly. Suddenly, Donny delivers a swift kick upwards.

Right there.

Right in the nads.

Branden clutches his now flaming regions, dropping to his knees as Donny lunges upwards and tackles him, straddling over him. He winds back and begins landing blow after blow on his unprotected face. The tables around Donny are chanting and cheering him on as Branden's face starts dripping blood like cherry water ice like a hot summer day.

Ah. Summer. The perfect season. No school. No Branden. No worries.

"HEY!"

The lunch hall monitor races over from across the room but isn't the most athletic person, so the circle of boys scatter past him, out of the lunch hall and race to their next class. He sees Dom walking through the hallway just outside the lunch hall, playing on his phone.

"Whatever you hear, I didn't start it!"

Donny races past him and up the stairs, slowing down as he sees Benny walking the walls, with a teacher walking towards Donny. Donny speeds up his walking and taps Benny on the shoulder.

"Yo wassup?"

Donny is catching his breath and trying to calm down as the boys dab each other up.

"Yo, I just kicked the shit out of Branden and got away with it."

"You beat up Branden? Where?"

"In the lunch hall. Mr. Dickinson was our lunch monitor."

"Dickinson? No wonder you got away with it. He makes Jonah Hill look thin. Goddamn it. You sixth lunch boys have all the fun."

The two boys chuckle at themselves and walk into their networking class. That class flew by too. A bunch of computer mumbo-jumbo crap. Never understood it. Never will. That class is a bore. Bell rang and Donny left for English class. 8th Period. Great way to close the day.

This is my forte.

"Okay, gentlemen. What is the main message behind Fahrenheit 451?"

A hand raises from the middle row.

"Donny?"

"Well, the message is that this particular dystopian society wants to survive but more importantly, thrive yet they are too busy wit the superficial happiness provided to'em, so they can not tackle wit ideas that are generated or made in their heads since they are distributed to them wit ease. But even those who seek to obtain better knowledge of their society, they cannot, due to the books bein illegal and if caught wit books, it's a crime."

"Excellent insight, Donny."

Donny fist bumps his Aidan and scribbles annotations into his book.

"How do you understand this? I haven't understood this book since we started it."

Donny sighs, looks at his book then peers at Aidan.

"I dunno. English is just my thing I guess."

Aidan shrugs as the rest of the class zips by. Time flies when you enjoy it. The bell rings at two thirty-nine and the classroom rumbles, with students stuffing papers and books into their bag and walking out of class.

"Remember guys, check your computers for homework. Have a good break. See you Monday!"

"You too Mr. P."

He gets out of class and walks out of school, texting Dom.

"Yo where you at?"

Donny waits a few seconds as he sees the three bubbles pop up on his screen.

"I got track practice today, I won't be home till 5ish. Take the twenty-eight home or wait till I'm done."

Donny sighs and shuts off his phone, putting it in his pocket. He walks down Solly, turns onto Rowland and walks down Rowland to the intersection, just barely catching the twenty-eight bus. He gets on the bus and it's just crowded with a sea of baby blue and red. All the seats were taken, so he just holds onto the bar, listening to music and playing on his phone, looking up occasionally, so he knows where to hop off.

The bus slows down and dumps a slew of Judge boys off at Rhawn and Verree, allowing Donny to take a seat. He rides the bus to the bank and hops off near the Dunkin Donuts on Oxford.

He crosses the intersection and walks down the street, smelling the fantastic smell of German meats as he pasts Rieker's. He walks past Semper Fi, looking through the window, watching the teachers set up for a class. The majestic smell of pizza hits his nose as he passes Joseph's, the doors open, letting the fresh, cool November air into the restaurant. He passes the auto shop and veers down the concrete pathway towards Wawa. He gets into Wawa and the place seems pretty busy. The Cecilia's and Fox Chase kids have gotten out and are indulging themselves in the delicacies of Wawa. He walks up to the tablet and gets the best meal that Wawa makes.

Buffalo chicken quesadilla.

He taps the screen to complete his order and watches as the printer spits out his order on the thin, little white paper. He rips it off the machine and walks over to the coolers and looks at the sodas.

My mom told me not to get sodas anymore, cause of this damn soda tax.

Donny peers at the soda, his mouth salivating at the look of a crisp, cold soda.

Ah fuck it.

He opens the door and grabs two sodas, walking over and waiting in line for the register, eventually making his way to it.

"How's it goin today?"

"Goin good."

The teen at the register sticks the scanner gun at the two sodas and the receipt, hearing three consecutive beeps.

"Nine dollars and eighty-six cents please."

Donny reaches into his wallet and pulls out a ten. He hands it to the cashier, who taps on the tablet, the cash drawer shooting out towards him. He places the ten into the drawer as the coins are spit out into the little dish.

"Have a good day!"

"You too."

Donny grabs the change from the little dish and walks back over to the food area, waiting away from the counter, staring at his phone. Footsteps in, out and around the restaurant batters his ears as he scrolls aimlessly through his phone. Suddenly, someone places a hand on his shoulder, causing Donny to turn abruptly, his peripheral flooded with purple and gold.

"DONNY!"

Shea pops out of nowhere and creeps up on Donny, making him jump but afterwards, the two boys chuckled and dabbed each other up.

"How you been Donny?"

"Doin good. Doin good . . . Did I tell you yet?"

Shea looks at Donny confused and shakes his head.

"I finally did it."

"Holy shit, you did it?"

Donny nods his head and blushes.

"Let's go!"

Shea dabs him up and throws an arm over his shoulder.

"Oh my God, I can't believe you did it. What happened?"

"I invited her to Aidan's last night, we went to the skate zone and then I took'er out to Steve's for some cheesesteaks."

"Steve's is the best. Good choice."

"I know, for real. Anyways, after we finished eatin, we were walkin back to my car and I held the door open, she got in and just as I was bout to close it, she tapped me on the back and I turned around, she pulled me in and kissed me."

"Ouuu."

Donny looks as his friend looks at him, nodding his head in respect.

"Anythin else?"

"Uhh . . . drove her back to'er place. Got out, walked'er to'er door and just as I was bout to leave, I turned around, walked up'er steps and we kissed."

Donny blushes and looks at his friend.

"Ouu, what did she say?"

"I cawled her beautiful and. . . she told me she loved me. And we made out on'er steps for a few minutes."

"Oh damn. Were'er folks home?"

Donny shakes his head.

"Damn. You should've done it."

Donny shakes his head.

"Nah. Definitely not on the first date. Besides, we're hangin out again on next Saturday night."

Shea nods and smiles at Donny.

"SEVENTY-SEVEN!"

Donny looks down at his receipt and sees that it's his number. He walks up to the counter, grabs his quesadilla and throws the paper into the basket.

"Thank you. Have a good day."

"Thank you. You too."

Donny follows Shea out of Wawa and walks down Oxford, turning into the Septa parking lot at Fox Chase Station. The two boys are indulging themselves in the exquisiteness of Wawa.

"So, how you been doin wit school?"

Donny takes a cool gulp of soda, feeling the sugary goodness rush through his veins.

Glp glp glp glp glp

Ahhhhhh

"I dunno man. Branden's been just gettin worse for some reason. I haven't done anythin."

"Oh no. What did you do?"

Donny sighs and takes another swig of soda.

"I got caught cheatin today, and Branden was in the dean's office and I was waitin outside of it. He left the office and I went in. As we passed each other, I stuck out my foot and tripped him. I got in a quick chuckle before gettin into the dean's office."

"Oof. Dickhead deserved it though."

"Exactly. Fast forward, I'm sittin at lunch. I hear him walk over to me and say '*Wassup faggot*' in'is big burly voice. I ignored him and kept on eatin my lunch. Then I heard'im say *'you listenin dickhead'* as he grabs my shoulder and rips me off my chair. He's standin over me and I'm on the ground and my God, he fuckin towered over me."

Shea's listening to Donny, not speaking as Donny reels him in with the suspension.

"So, Whatchu do next?"

"I kicked him. Right in the nuts. He grabbed'em and dropped right to'is knees. While he was on'is knees, I lunged at'im, knockin'im on the ground. I straddled over'im and just started layin'im out. I hit'im in the chin, the nose, the jaw, the eyes, I was beatin the livin shit outta him. The lunch hall monitor hears the fightin, after bout ten seconds and starts runnin over. This monitor isn't the healthiest human bein in the world, so everyone just scattered, leavin Branden bleedin snot outta his nose on the lunch hall floor."

"Goddamn. And ya didn't get caught?"

Donny smiles and shakes his head.

"Jesus. You think Branden'll get back at you?"

Donny smirks and nods as he takes a swig of soda.

"Oh yeah. I'm just waitin for him to do somethin. I'm sure it'll happen soon."

Shea nods and takes a swig of his drink. They walked through the Fox Chase Rec and down to Verree.

"Well, here's where we part ways. See ya soon Donny."

"See ya Shea."

The two boys dab each other up and part their ways, Shea walking down Verre toward Quig's, Donny turning down Rhawn and walking towards his home down Rising Sun. Donny gets inside his house and shuts the door. Donny looks at his living room and sees Lissy sitting on the couch, eating a bowl of cereal, still in her Ryan uniform.

"Sup loser."

Lissy keeps her eyes fixed on the TV and gives Donny the middle finger, who swiftly gives her one back. He walks into the dining room and plops his Wawa bag onto the table.

"Hey Donny."

"Hey Ma."

Donny takes his quesadilla out of the bag and sits down at the table, tearing into the delicious food ravenously.

"How was school today?"

"It was . . ."

Donny swallows, so he doesn't talk through mouthfuls of food.

"It was good."

"Anythin interestin happen today?"

Donny, caught by surprise, swallows too quickly and chokes on his food, feeling the buffalo sauce sear his throat. After clearing his throat, he takes a swig of soda to soothe it.

"No. Nuthin interestin at all."

Donny starts sweating but realizing his mother has no clue what he's talking about, he wipes his brow and calms down.

"Dom had practice today?"

Donny nods his head as he sinks his teeth into the buffalo chicken-y goodness.

My God, this tastes delicious.

"It's five, so he should be home soon."

Donny's mom nods her head and walks into the kitchen.

"You got homework tonight?"

"Nah. I did it wit the teacher in class."

I didn't do anything in class. I'm tired after today's encounters with Branden. I just need a nap.

"I'm tired Ma. I'm goin to bed."

"Okay. Goodnight."

He walks to the kitchen, tosses the trash out and walks upstairs, goes into his room and lies down on his bed.

Bzzz bzzz.

'Heyyy.'

Donny smiles and opens his phone, replying to her text.

'Heyy.'

'What's up?'

'Nothing much. Just laying in bed, playing on my phone.'

'Me too. I'm really bored.'

'Feel that.'

'Hey, I was checking my schedule and was wondering if you were down to hang out next Saturday?'

'Absolutely. Next Saturday sounds perfect.'

Donny smiles at his phone, the feeling of her lips still tingling throughout his body.

'*I'm excited for next Saturday.*'

'*Me too <3.*'

Erin smiles at Donny's texts, her body becoming warm and her heart becoming giddy as she lies on her bed.

'*Whatchu wanna do?*'

Donny looks at her text, ponders for a second and then responds.

'*Idk. Whatchu feel like?*'

'*I was thinking maybe Italian. Maybe Olive Garden, if you're down and then Nifty's afterwards for dessert?*'

'*Absolutely.*'

Donny smiles at his phone as the three bubbles pop up.

'*And then . . . my place after? To meet my parents and hang out after dessert!*'

'Yeah. Absolutely.'

'Awesome. I got some homework to take care of right now. I'll talk to you later Donny.'

'Talk to ya later, Erin ;)'

Erin shuts off her phone and falls back in her bed, closing her eyes and smiles.

I hope he's good.

Donny shuts off his bedroom light and rolls to his side, watching videos on his computer.

Damn she's beautiful.

I hope we click.

. . .

Donny's out to eat with his family and he looks around the table, his father donned in a fancy suit and his mother in a beautiful dress.

The hell am I in a tux for?

He peers over at his siblings, both of them dressed very nicely.

"Congratulations Donny. Senior's year's over buddy."

Donny looks at his father, Donny's gaze a look of pure confusion.

"What's all this for?"

His father looks at him and laughs, baffled by his son's question.

"What do you mean 'what's all this for?' It's your graduation party."

His father, beaming a look of happiness, raises his cheap restaurant brew and stands up, his family following suit.

"To Donny."

"TO DONNY!"

The family toast their son, all taking a swig of their drink, Donny taking a sip of his water, still wondering what's going on. Suddenly, Donny looks up and sees his father's nice white dress shirt start sprouting a red liquid, the shirt blotting up the liquid more and more. Donny's father looks down at his hand, now dripping with blood. His father, now in a dead stare at Donny, whispes as loud as a silent shout.

"Not my sons."

Donny's father falls towards the table with the heavy weight of his body as just as his body hits the table dead, Donny awakes from his hallucinatory nightmare. He looks around the room, pitch black but silent. His body is covered in sweat but also shivering, Donny's teeth chattering loudly in the cold silence of his bedroom.

Donny turns in his bed and slams his elbow into the bedframe, causing a painful end to his terrifying nightmare. He cracks his neck and looks around the room.

Still dark.

He listens intently.

Dom's asleep. What time is it?

Donny looks at his phone, screen face down on his bed. He flips it over and reads the time.

Two a.m.? What the fuck?

Donny rubs his eyes and looks through his phone notifications, seeing if there was anything important.

'*Heyy Donny.*'

Sent 9:51 p.m.

'*Hello?*'

Sent 10:04 p.m.

'*Donnnnnyyyy . . .*'

Sent 10:35 p.m.

'I think you passed out. I'll talk to you tomorrow Donny. Sweet dreams. Love ya. Goodnight!'

Sent 11:06 p.m.

Donny sighs heavily and shuts his phone off. He looks around the room and hearing Dom asleep, he gets up and gets out of bed, walking over to his bureau. He reaches inside his dresser and grabs a pair of socks. He unrolls the socks to reveal a vape.

It ain't Ports. But it'll do for now.

He rolls the socks back up and sits down on the top bunk of his bed. He brings it to his mouth and breathes in, feeling the vapor becoming denser and denser inside his mouth. He pulls it away and inhales, holding his breath. He waits as he feels the nicotine-filled vapor plunges deep into the depths of his lungs, filling the veins and sending nicotine to his brain. After a few seconds, he exhales, tasting the blueberry flavor on his lips and inside his cheeks, falling on his back, feeling the rush of nicotine fly through his body, giving him a deep buzz. He rips it and rips it until he passes out with the vape still in his hand. All he can see is Erin in his buzzed, sleep-filled state.

I love you.

He turns his body, throws his sheets over him and falls asleep peacefully.

Today was a good day.

VI

Donny wakes up and rolls over in his bed.

Ten o'clock.

Thank God I turned my alarm off.

Donny walks out of his room and after relieving himself in the bathroom, walks downstairs to his sister and mother intently watching the Thanksgiving Day Parade.

They still watch that dumbass parade?

Donny shakes his head as he walks past them and into the kitchen. He opens the cupboard and grabs some cereal. He places the box on the counter and walks over to the cabinet and grabs a bowl, looking at the Phillies helmet ice cream bowls in the back of the cabinet. He chuckles at them, laughing because they still have them from ten years ago.

His first ball game.

The stadium was packed. The Phils were playing the Marlins, back when they were still the Florida Marlins and not those stupid Miami Marlins. The game was back and forth the entire time. I loved the whole infield, from Rollins to Howard to Utley. But my favorite of them all was the catcher. Number fifty-one. Carlos Ruiz. Chooch. I love playing catcher for my rec league but I love watching Chooch play even more. It came down to the bottom of the ninth. Bases loaded as Harry Kalas' voice rang throughout Citizens Bank Park like the voice of God.

"Number Fifty-one . . . CARLOOOOOOS RUIZ!"

The count quickly went to one and one. The next pitch was smacked right up the middle to the shortstop as the runner sprinted home and won the game. Walk-off single. Six to five. Chooch for the win. My dad, my brother and me all screamed in excitement as the Phillies dugout emptied and stormed after Ruiz, surrounding him in a dog pile. That was one of the best moments of my life, only to be surpassed the following year by the Phils winning it all. The Big One. The World Series. Now, if only the damn Birds could win us one.

Donny walks out of the kitchen and sits in the living room, eating his cereal as his Mom and Lissy watch the television intently. He rolls his eyes and goes onto his phone, waiting till the parade is over to turn on the football games. A couple minutes pass and Dom stumbles down the steps slowly. He peers over at the television and groans loudly, walking into the kitchen, away from the stupidity of the parade. The hours pass by and the show's finally done. His mother goes into the kitchen, washes her bowl out and walks into the living room.

"Before you three can do anythin, you need to just straighten up your rooms before everyone comes over."

All three kids groan loudly but reluctantly go up the steps and clean their rooms. After a couple hours of cleaning their rooms and the house, the two boys and their father sit down to watch the game. They already missed the first game and the second one is Chargers versus Cowboys, so they're Chargers fans for Thanksgiving because fuck the Cowboys.

The family is supposed to start arriving at five thirty but there's always someone who has to come forty-five minutes early. The turkey's in the oven. Mom's in the kitchen making mashed potatoes and stuffing. They have enough canned corn to feed an Army platoon, cranberry sauce a plenty and croissants that taste like heaven on a plate. Plus Jamie's coming. It's gonna be a nice Thanksgiving.

Surprisingly, no one came early. Five thirty comes and the family starts flowing in. Donny and Dom are waiting for their cousin, Jamie, to come over. The family is just sitting on the couch, watching the game as Donny looks up at the clock, reading quarter after six. His mother cries into the living room,

"Dinner's ready!"

Donny's Dad grabs the TV remote, turns it off and walks into the dining room. Just as the family's sitting down, a knock on the door echoes through the house. Donny walks over to the door and opens it.

"JAMIE!"

"EY! Wassup guys!"

James Ronald Mooney, or Jamie, is Donny's cousin, a little older than Dom. The oldest son of Donny's uncle on his dad's side, he's a junior in college at Temple. Dom and Jamie will be on the same campus next year. They'll fuck some shit up. You just know it. One Mooney boy is crazy enough, two is even more wild.

He walks in the door as the family gets up to say hi to him. Dom walks over and dabs him up.

"Wassup Jamie."

As the two boys bro-hug it out, Dom whispers something into his ear. Jamie listens and nods his head, smiling as they pull away. Donny's dad walks over to Jamie and gives him a firm handshake.

"Ya hungry Jamie?"

"Always, Uncle Drew."

Donny's dad smiles and the boys and Jamie all walk over to the dining room table, crammed with twelve people in it and all the younger kids in the living room. After a quick prayer, the Mooney family quickly begins indulging themselves in the dinner presented before them. The turkey, juicy and cooked to perfection, the mashed potatoes more creamy and smoother than silk and the croissants more air-y than a cloud.

It was your normal Irish Thanksgiving dinner. Lots of food. Lots of politics. Lots of yelling and of course, lots *and lots* of alcohol. So much alcohol, the three boys were able to snag some teas and beers while the adults weren't paying attention.

After finishing their food and wiping their faces of the remnants, Dom and Jamie went into the living room, sitting down and watching the game as Donny brough all the dishes into the kitchen. After dinner is finished, Donny's mother stands up, still donning her Thanksgiving-themed apron.

"Who wants dessert? We got ice cream, pumpkin pie and apple pie."

The young kids in the living room, who barely even finished their dinner, all scream 'I DO!' at the top of their lungs. Everyone at the dining room table nod their heads semi-drunkenly as they grab their plates and place them in the sink. After having dessert, Donny walks into the kitchen where his mother is cleaning the dishes.

"Hey Mom. I'll do the dishes for you."

Donny's mother turns around and looks at him, staring at him with a look.

"What do you want?"

Donny's face turns red as he places the dishes into the sink.

"Jamie wants to go for a walk wit me and Dom, so we could tawk and catch up. Could we go after I do the dishes?"

His mother gives him a look but nods her head. Smiling, Donny quickly takes care of the dinner and dessert dishes. After finishing cleaning them, he walks into the living room, where his brother and cousin are playing on their phones.

"You guys ready?"

The two boys nod and make their way to the door.

"We'll be back in a few. See ya guys."

The three boys leave the house and walk down the sidewalk towards Rhawn. Jamie opens his backpack, now filled with seven to eight cans of beer and tea. The twilight sky shining down on them, Jamie ruffles with his pockets and nods afterwards.

"You know where a spot is, Dom?"

Dom nods as they walk down Rhawn, turning onto Tabor, walking towards the trails. Once they enter, they find a bench and sit down on it. Jamie pulls a small sandwich bag full of weed nuggets and some Backwoods he got at Wawa on the way to their house. Dom reaches into his bag and grabs a can for each boy.

"It's good stuff too."

Jamie grinds the nugs down, takes the wrapper and rolls it up, slathering it with saliva to seal it closed. He pulls out a cheap lighter and lights it up, breathing in and watching as the smoke engulfs in his lungs as the two boys crack open their cold ones.

Dom and Donny watch as their cousin breathes out heavily, watching the weed smoke dissipate in the cold winter air. He passes it to Dom, who takes a few drags, coughing after the first hit. Dom then passes it to Donny, who takes a long drag, watching the end of the blunt ember up as he breathes in longer and longer. Finally, he breathes out, coughing sporadically and incessantly.

"Jeez, calm down there Donny. Another hit like that, I'mma have to take you to the fuckin hospital."

Donny looks at his cousin and nods, a smile slowly stretching across his face.

Oh yeah. I'm fried.

The two boys pass it around until the blunt is just about finished. Jamie takes the last hit and tosses it into the asphalt trail. The three boys stand up and walk out of the trails, hoodies draped over their heads and eyes bloodshot.

"Ey, do I look high?"

Donny lifts his hoodie up as Jamie tilts his head down to look at him in the eyes.

"Oh yeah. You're fucked bro."

Donny's paranoia starts to kick in as they round the corner of Ripley and walk to their house. They walk up the steps as Dom turns around, eyes more red than a Phils Cap.

"Just keep it cool Donny. You'll be aight ya know."

The three boys walk into the house, the family intently watching the Thanksgiving day football games on NBC. Donny walks into the kitchen, his mind still vibrantly fried from the blunt and gets a cup of soda. Hoodie still on, he sits down on the couch and starts drinking his soda. His dad is shouting at the television, letting the refs know how terrible their calls are. He looks down at his phone and sees a text from Erin.

'Heyy.'

'Hey Erin.'

'I'm high rn.'

Donny is smiling as he watches the three bubbles bounce on his phone.

'Good for you.'

'Yeah. My cousin had some bud on him. We smoked it all.'

'Cool . . .'

Donny stares at his phone, waiting for Erin to respond. After a few minutes of blacking out, he realizes that she already responded.

Shiiit. I'm high high.

'Happy Thanksgiving. Hope yours went well.'

'Happy Thanksgiving to you too, Donny. Love you.'

'I love you too.'

"DONNY!"

His mother's cry from the kitchen snapped out of his high almost immediately and he got up and walked into the kitchen.

"Wassup Mom?"

"You forgot to wash the turkey pan."

Donny looks up at his mother, avoiding eye contact, since he feels like his eyes are drier than the Sahara Desert.

"I'll take care of it Mom. After that, Can I go to bed? I'm really tired."

His mother nods at him and Donny starts cleaning the turkey pan. After a few minutes, he grabs some paper towels and dries it clean.

"Done mom."

"Okay. Say goodbye to your family."

Dony walks over to all of his cousins, aunts and uncles. He walks over to Jamie and gives him a bro-hug.

"Thanks for tonight. It was much needed."

"Absolutely kid. See ya soon."

Jamie gets up and hugs Donny's mom.

"See ya, Aunt Beth."

Jamie shakes his uncle's hands firmly, looking right into his eyes, smiling happily.

"See ya, Uncle Drew. It was a pleasure bein here wit youse guys."

See ya Jamie. Safe drive home."

Jamie nods as Dom stands up and bro-hugs him.

"See ya soon Jamie."

"Absolutely."

Jamie walks out the door and down the block, hopping in his pickup truck and drives away, his taillights disappearing in the dark November night.

"Aight. Night Mom. Night Dad."

Donny walks over and gives both of his parents a hug, walking up the stairs and into his room after saying goodnight to them. He rolls onto his bed and throws the covers over him, feeling his body become warm and bubbly, mostly because of the high but it was warm under the covers too. He plugs his earbuds in and listens to Uzi and Meek, as the music is blasting into his head as he slowly drifts to sleep.

    Today was a good day.

VII

As soon as Donny woke up, he knew something bad was gonna happen today. Break was over. Monday came so fast. Faster than he ever expected. He went through his normal morning routine. Get out of bed, get dressed, grab lunch and leave. He hops in the car with Dom and they start on their way to school.

"Yo Donny?"

Donny peers up from his phone to answer his brother's question.

"Yeoo?"

"What did you mean by what you said last week?"

Donny sighs and shuts his phone off.

"You can't tell Mom or Dad . . ."

"Okay. I won't tell."

Donny breathes in deeply, staring at his brother directly in the eyes.

"I got in a fight durin lunch."

"Wit who? We both have 6th lunch."

"It was wit Branden. He pulled me off my seat and stood over me, so I kicked'im in the nuts and he dropped to'is knees, but I was so pissed off, I just started beatin the livin shit outta'im."

"An you didn't get caught?"

"Dickinson was the lunch hall monitor."

Dom shoots Donny a look and nods his head.

"It must've started as you were leavin the lunch hall cause it was like thirty seconds long. He threw me to the ground, I kicked'im, tackled'im and then I laid'im out. I sprinted outta there once Dickinson saw everyone. Cause you weren't that far down the hall when I was sprintin outta there."

Dom nods his head as he passes over the bridge towards Cresco. They get into the parking lot and park the car.

"Just don't get into trouble today, okay?"

Donny nods and both get out of the car and into school. Donny walks over to Benny and Aidan, who are staring at Donny and smiling wildly.

"Yo, we heard whatchu did. That's fuckin wild, Donny"

Donny shoots his friends a nervous smile and grabs his bag, taking out his notebook.

"Do either of youse got the homework for geometry class and theology?"

"I got both of'em."

Aidan reaches into his book bag and grabs two notebooks, opening them to the homework needed for the class.

"Thanks, bro."

Donny grabs the notebooks and starts scribbling down the homework answers, listening to music and writing answer after answer into his notebook, only to be interrupted by the homeroom bell.

"I pass you in the halls. I'll give this to you then. And you can give me my stuff in the bathroom durin third?"

Aidan nods as Donny gives him a handful of cash and the boys part their ways to their different homerooms. Donny walks into his homeroom class, plops the two notebooks on his desk and continues writing notes and copying answers.

He gets through the theology homework and is getting through the geometry homework, just as he looks up and sees the clock hit five after eight and the bell rings throughout the school. He grabs the notebooks and heads to his first period. He's walking through the hall to get to his bio class. He sits down as the teacher walks in, with a stack of paper about four or five inches thick

"Okay gentlemen. We got a quiz today. I'll give you five minutes to study before we begin. Go!"

Donny looks up at the teacher in a state of shock.

We have a quiz today? Are you fuckin kiddin me?

Donny shakes his head at the teacher and continues with his notes. He spends all five minutes writing his notes, finishing them just as the teacher is passing out the quiz.

Whatever. I have an eighty for the class. If I bomb the quiz, I'll be fine.

She hands Donny the quiz paper. Fifteen multiple choice questions. Donny rolls his eyes and just goes down the quiz.

ABCDE repeat.

He takes all of ten seconds to complete the quiz and he hands it in. He walks back to his desk and sits down, slumping in his chair. The teacher gives Donny a perplexed look and grabs the quiz off the teacher's desk. She looks at his quiz for a few seconds and sighs loudly.

"Mr. Mooney?"

Donny, who's staring at his desk, scribbling on it with pencil, looks up at his teacher.

"Yes Mrs. G?"

"See me after class please."

Donny nods his head somberly, to make it seem like he cares but quite frankly, he doesn't give a damn. Bio class goes by incredibly slow, as Donny watches his classmates hand in their quizzes, one by one. He looks up at the clock, it reading eight fifty.

He lays his head down on his arms and takes a quick nap, waiting for his ears to be beaten with the noise of the period bell. After a few minutes, the sound hits his ears and he gets up to leave class. He walks to the teacher's desk and waits for her to finish gathering the quizzes.

"Mr. Mooney, why'd you do this?"

Donny looks at his quiz, with the order ABCDE repeating three times, chuckling at it silently.

"Cause I didn't study. I have class, can I go now?"

Donny smirks at her and turns around.

"Mr. Mooney, I'll fail you for the quarter if this happens again."

Donny looks at her, shrugs and sighs, walking out of her classroom and to his second period, the hallway busy with the bustle of students walking to their classes. He sees Aidan walking towards him and Donny takes out the two notebooks, giving them back to Aidan.

"Ay thanks Donny."

"No problem, Aidan."

The two boys dab each other up and continue walking to their classes. He's walking down the hall and he sees Dom and his friends but doesn't see Branden.

"Ay wassup Donny."

All of Dom's friends dab Donny up and for a second, Donny's actually happy to be at school.

No Branden. Guess he's out sick today.

He gets to his third period class and places his bag on his desk.

"Can I go to the bathroom real quick?"

The teacher nods and Donny walks out of his classroom, down the hall and to the bathroom. As he walks in, he sees a pair of shoes under the stalls. He walks over to the urinal and after spending a few minutes relieving himself, he waits outside the stall that has the kid in it. He hears the flush of the toilet and the large figure emerges from the stall.

"Wassup Aidan, You got the jawns?"

"Oh, yeah."

Aidan reaches into his pocket and pulls out a pack of pods for Donny's vape and also a pack of cigs. Aidan pulls out his own vape and places it inside of his mouth.

"Sweet. Thanks Aidan. I gave you the cash already right?"

Aidan rips the vape and exhales, nodding his head.

"Yeah, you have it to me this mornin."

Aidan takes a rip and passes it to Donny, who takes a couple rips before handing it back.

"I gotta get to class. Thanks for the rips and for my jawns."

"No problem. Anytime."

The two boys dab each other up and part their ways. Donny's walking back to class, still feeling the buzz from the rips as a large figure emerges from one of the classrooms.

Oh shit. It's Branden.

He spots Donny and makes a beeline for him. Donny doesn't move. He just stands there. Watching Branden come closer and closer to him.

"Wassup faggot."

Donny looks up at Branden as he stands in front of him, towering over Donny.

"I'm sick and tired of you, little Mooney. I'm gonna kill you."

Donny, unfazed, mocks him.

"Where and when, dickhead?"

Branden, taken aback from Donny's response, becomes fuming mad, with Donny seeing his face turn a blood-boiling red color.

"Bridge. Tomorrow night."

"I'll be there."

Donny walks down the hall towards his classroom before Branden shouts at him.

"Ay Mooney?"

Donny turns around and looks at him with a smirk.

"After tomorrow night, the next time your family will see you is on fuckin Action News!"

Donny gives him the finger, turns around and immediately, his face goes white.

Shit. What did you just get yourself into Donny?

He walks into the classroom and after that, the day just seems like speed by. He didn't do anything. Didn't take notes. Didn't pay attention in class. Didn't eat lunch. He heard the bell ring at the end of school. He got onto the twenty-eight and went home.

"Wassup Los-"

"Shut up Lissy."

Donny walks upstairs and lies on his bed, contemplating what he'd done today.

I'm gonna get the shit kicked outta me.

Donny pulls his phone out and turns it on, going to his messages.

'*Hey Erin.*'

Donny exits out of his messages and starts playing some dumb phone game until he sees her notification pop up at the top of his screen.

'Hey Donny.'

'How's your day been?'

'Been pretty good so far. Swamped with homework but pretty good.'

'Cool. Can I tell you something and it has to be a secret?'

Donny feels his heart rate pick up as he watches the three bubbles pop up on his phone.

'Absolutely. You got my promise. It's safe with me.'

Donny breathes heavily as he types the words on his phone.

'I'm fighting a senior tomorrow night and he's probably gonna beat the life outta me, so when I come to

your house on Saturday, I might have some bruises but I'll be okay.'

'Oh my God, Donny, don't go to the fight. What the hell is wrong with you?'

'I told him where and when he wanted to fight and he said bridge tomorrow night.'

'And I didn't back down. So I'm fighting him tomorrow night.'

'Oh my God Donny, please don't do it.'

Donny stares at the texts, wondering how to respond. After a few minutes, he responds.

'You're right. I won't do it. No matter what he says, I'll call it off.'

'Thank you Donny. I care about you. I just want you to be safe.'

'I know. I understand. I got some homework to take care of. I'll talk to you later Erin. Can't wait to see you Saturday night. I love you. Talk to you later.'

'Can't wait to see you again. I love you too Donny. See ya <3'

Donny shuts off his phone and lays his head down, as tears start streaming down his face. He opens his phone, goes to his DMs and messages Branden.

'Just you and me tomorrow night. No bullshit. Just you and me.'

He watches his messages for a few minutes, staring at it as the three bubbles pop up.

'Whatever you want, little Mooney. Be ready to get your ass kicked faggot.'

Donny shuts his phone off and rolls over in his bed. After staring at his ceiling for a few minutes, he looks at his clock, reading it five fifty-eight. He gets out of bed and walks downstairs to eat dinner with his family.

Tonight is Taco Tuesday. My mom always makes tacos on Tuesday. They're always the best.

He grabs a plate and walks up behind Lissy, waiting to get food.

"Wassup Loser."

Donny looks at his sister and smiles at her.

"I'm sorry that for every time I've hurt you, Lissy. It won't happen again. I'm sorry."

Lissy looks at her brother, confused.

"The hell's gotten into you?"

Lissy grabs her tacos and walks into the living room. Donny grabs his tacos and walks into the dining room, where his mother and father are sitting. The screen door opens and a lock turns, with Dom coming in the door from track practice.

"Hey Dom."

Dom throws his book bag on the floor and walks into the kitchen, grabbing a plate and getting dinner.

Dom plunges his mouth into the taco, chewing and swallowing the meaty delicious food.

"Practice was good. I got another meet on Sunday."

"Where's it at and what time on Sunday?"

Dom, thinking for a second, pulls out his phone and looks at the schedule.

"It's a Lehigh University and we gotta be there at two o'clock for warm-ups."

"Two at Lehigh? But the Birds are playin against the Lions. We're gonna crush'em."

"I'm sorry but I gotta meet at two."

Donny's Dad sighs but agrees to driving Dom to his track meet. Donny finishes his food, throws the dirty dishes in the sink and walks out of the kitchen. He walks over to his parents to give them hugs.

"Got a lotta homework tonight, I need to finish it and then I'm goin to bed."

Donny's mother stands up from her seat to give her son a hug.

"Goodnight Donny."

"I love you Mom."

He lets go of his mother and turns to his father.

"Night Dad."

"Night Donny."

Just as his dad pulls away from him, he squeezes him a little harder.

"Love you Dad."

His dad, caught off guard from Donny's sudden hug, hugs him back even harder.

"I love you too Donny. Don't forget that."

Donny feels his face welling up with tears but restrains them from coming out. He walks upstairs and goes into his bureau, grabbing his vape. He puts in a new pod and rips it endlessly, his body becoming numb to the feeling of the buzz. He lies on his bed and goes onto his phone.

'Hey Erin, I feel really sick. I'll text you tomorrow. Goodnight.'

He shuts his phone off and stares at his ceiling, his vape now empty in his hands from the constant usage. He takes it to his bathroom, wraps the vape and the empty pods in a ball of toilet paper and tosses it in the bathroom trash can. He goes into his book bag and pulls out his pack of new pods and the pack of cigs. He opens his bedroom window and looks at the pack of pods, chucks them out of his room, watching them land in his neighbor's yard across from the driveway. He shuts the window and gets on the top bunk, laying down, feeling tears rush down his face and sadness consumes him till he falls asleep.

Today was horrible.

VIII

Today didn't even feel real. Two forty comes in a flash and eventually, Donny gets kicked out of school and has to leave because it's five o'clock. He gets out of school and starts walking down Solly, stopping and peering at the majestic baseball field in the early December sunset. He stares at the fields, running his eyes across the green grass and the blue strips running up the foul lines. In the not so far off distance, he can see the goalposts and the nets behind them on the football and soccer field.

He turns and walks down Crispin, his eyes watching his feet take their steps, not even paying attention to what is ahead of him cause what's ahead doesn't matter.

Only right now does.

He walks down the street till he's right behind the goalpost, staring at the glistening field in the early evening glow. He breathes in deep and lets out a heavy sigh. He looks down at his phone.

Seven thirty. Forty-five till the fight.

He walks around the fields, circling around, taking his sweet old time. He walks over to the playground right next to school and finds a stray basketball just laying on the court. He picks it up and drops his book bag, just shooting shots, feeling the stress of everything fade away as he shoots the ball again.

And again.

And again.

Losing track of time, he just keeps playing till the sunset is forever gone, the moon his only friend. He picks up his bag and walks to Bridge. He opens his phone and scrolls through his apps to his messages. Slowly, he clicks on her name and starts typing.

'I love you Erin. Always remember it. Never forget it.'

He hits send and watches as the message sends to Erin. He sees the three bubbles pop up shortly after sending the message but shuts the phone completely off, watching the screen go black in his hands. He keeps walking through the trails, seeing a little rudimentary fire going, made of small twigs and paper. It's pitch black, so all Donny can see is fire and Branden's silhouette in the moonlight standing next to it. His mind hears twigs snapping and leaves being ruffled in the woods.

Worry about him and him alone.

He walks over to the fire and drops his book bag next to it.

"Didn't think you'd show up, little Mooney. And you're still in your fuckin unifrom? Whatta faggot!"

Branden starts laughing at Donny, who looks down at himself in his uniform and blushes. He walks up near Branden, eyes fixed on his nose, bandaged from last Monday's incident. He reaches into his pocket and pulls out the pack of cigs he got from Aidan and tosses them at Branden, who snags the carton from the air.

"What's this?"

"I know you smoke'em a lot. I don't wanna fight you. I apologize for beatin you up in the lunch hall."

Branden takes a few seconds to look at the pack, the '1913' staring back at him under the thin plastic cover wrapped around the pack.

"These are my favorite brand."

Donny nods somberly, and for a brief second, Branden smiles at him.

After a few seconds, Branden's face turns from a smile to a look of pure malice.

"Now there's enough for all of us."

"What?"

"GET'IM!"

Branden pulls a knife out from his pocket, flicks it open and stabs Donny right in the stomach. Donny feels the clean metal blade sink into him, his body becoming warm and numb as he stumbles backwards, the air knocked out of him.

A group of boys emerge from the darkness of the Pennypack woods, wielding pipes and bats. Branden backs away and laughs maliciously as Donny falls to his knees, quickly feeling the harsh, coarse wood connect with his face as if the boy were swinging for the fences.

He falls to his side, immediately feeling the blood rush out of his nose and mouth. The boys jump him, battering and assaulting Donny with blows and kicks and punches. In one instance, he feels the blade fall out of his stomach and fall into the dirt, feeling as if his intestines are oozing from his stomach m.

He curls up into a ball, feeling a warm red liquid spill from his head and stomach, his body growing limp and numb. Donny can feel the cuts and bruises being formed. After a few minutes of the tortuous beatings, Branden shouts at the boys, who disperse away from

Donny, leaving the boy whimpering and bleeding his life away in the dirt.

Branden kneels over Donny's near lifeless body and smirks. He sees the knife on the ground a couple feet away. He stands up, walks over to it and picks it up, bringing it over to Donny. He leans over him and grabs him by his Judge tee, the 'FJ' now drenched in blood and dirt, and pulls Donny towards his face.

"Told ya you were gonna end up on Action News."

He takes the knife and plunges it deep into Donny's chest, twisting it slowly as Donny whimpers painfully in his hands.

I'm sorry. I love you.

Donny's muscles become loose and his joints painless. His body drifts away slowly. His mind becomes a blur.

Drinking. Smoking. Wiffle ball. Smoking. Breakfast. Erin. Shea. Basketball. Erin. Mass. Aidan. Friends. Erin. Skate Zone. Steve's. Erin. The kiss . . . The kiss . . . *The Kiss*. School. Branden. Cheating. The fight. School. Vaping. Cigarettes. Branden. The Fight. Apologies. *I love you. Don't forget it.* The Fight. The Fight. The Fight. Fire. Branden. Cigarettes. Knife. Pain. Bats. Pipes. Punches. Pain. Kicks. Blood. Bruises. Pain. Pain. Pain.

I'm sorry.

Donny's eyes flicker with death and his body turns heavy. Branden drops his lifeless corpse into the dirt. He puts the fire out and washes his hands in the creek.

Branden was right.

Donny ended up on Action News.

IX

Good evening, I'm John Gardener. And I'm Cecila Tyson. Breaking news tonight of a teenage boy found dead near Pennypack Bridge. His body was found mutilated, covered in bruises, with two stab wounds, one to the stomach and one to his chest. The teen also had numerous broken bones, with metallic flakes and wooden splinters embedded all over his body. When police arrived on scene, the boy was still in his school uniform, his wallet and phone still on him. The police identified him as Donald Mooney, a junior at Father Judge High School, just a few minutes away from the scene of the crime. We will keep you updated on anything regarding the murder of Donald Mooney.

. . .

Dom was sitting in the back of the rectory. His body was numb yet overridden with sadness. He waited until he was alone. The tears became overwhelming. He hears the door to the rectory open and his mother, his father and Lissy walk in. They see Dom and immediately rush over to him, hugging him as he keels over in pain, anguish and sadness. His tears stream down his face incessantly, soaking into his tie. After a few minutes, he wipes his face of the tears. He walks to the back of the church, the doorway flooded with family members, relatives, friends and classmates.

Dom puts on the pall bearer's glove and grabs the casket, carrying his brother's body up the aisle, his face stout but the tears running. He places the casket on the bier and sits down next to his parents. Lissy walked up to the altar, donning a black floor-length dress, tears streaming down her face uncontrollably.

"I'm sorry Donny. I'm sorry. I wish I could apologize in person. I'm sorry Donny."

Aidan, Benny, Paulie and Ricky, impressively dressed in suits and ties, all walk up to the altar, staring at the top of the casket, faces wet from the tears.

Benny breaks down, audibly letting out a cry of pain. Aidan puts an arm around his shoulder, pulling him tight as tears run down his face faster.

Shea walks over to Mister and Misses Mooney, with visible tears on his face as he looks at Donny's parents, writhing with grief.

"I'm sorry, Mister and Misses Mooney. He was the best. I'm gonna miss'im."

Dom barely remembers the funeral. All he remembers is the eulogy, given by his mother and the casket being lowered into the grave.

He remembers the feelings of pain and sadness. He remembers going home after the funeral, walking to his room and looking at the top bunk, knowing it will always be empty.

He remembers laying in bed and hearing a knock on his bedroom door and seeing Lissy come in, with tears streaming down her face. He motions for her to come towards him and they both hug, crying on each other's shoulders, feeling the sadness rush over them unbearably in this moment of sibling embrace. A pain Dom would hold with him for the rest of his life.

Dom remembers everything. And as he told his baby brother as he watched the dirt being dumped on the shiny metallic casket,

"I'm gonna find him. I promise Donny. I promise baby brother. I promise."

Dom remembers going to school two weeks later, the first time since it happened. He remembers the sight of Branden in the hallways at school. And he remembers the DM that started it all . . .

'Yo Branden.'

'Wassup Dom.'

'I'm looking for cigs. Can I get some from you? I'm just trying to deal with the pain.'

'Yeah I gotchu. I'm sorry for what happened. My condolences.'

'Meet me under Pennypack Bridge at like seven. I got practice and shit like that. I'll bring the money for two packs.'

'Okay. I'll bring two packs.'

'See ya then.'

Dom turns his phone off. He walks downstairs and sees his father asleep on the couch watching a movie. His mother is working overnight tonight as a nurse. He walks into his parents' bedroom and opens his father's closet. He reaches for the top shelf of the closet, riffling his hand around until feeling the cold touch of metal. He grabs it and pulls it from the shelf, staring at the shiny metal of his father's .38 special revolver. He reaches up again and grabs the box of ammo. He puts the gun inside his pocket. He brings it into his room and tosses it in his bureau drawer, not thinking about it, his frantic mind having peace for a moment as he drifts to sleep.

He wakes up for school and grabs the pistol from his bureau and places it in his book bag. Once in his car, he takes it out and tosses it into his glove compartment.

The school day passes. Two thirty-nine arrives in an instant. Dom doesn't even go to practice that day. He sat in his car, staring at a picture of Donny for hours on end.

After everyone left the parking lot, he opened the glove compartment. He looks at the gun, shining in the brightly lit dusk sky and then his baby brother's picture. Tears start running down his face. He doesn't stop them. He doesn't care. He puts the picture down and one by one, he loads the bullets into the cylinder, fumbling with them through tear-filled eyes. Time flies by as the tears flow harder and harder. He stares at the picture of his baby brother and screams as loud as he can, letting out all of his pain.

All of his sadness.

All of his anger.

He looks at his phone, it reading eight thirty. He grabs the picture of Donny, kisses it and places it into his pocket. He grabs the pistol and sticks it down into his waistband by the small of his back. He walks down the Pennypack trails and sees the shadow of Branden in the distance. He comes a little closer and sees for certain that it is Branden.

"Wassup Dom."

Dom, his anger growing, dabs him up with an expressionless look.

"You got'em?"

Branden reaches inside his jacket pocket and pulls out the two packs of cigs.

"Yeah I got'em."

Immediately, Dom snaps.

"I'm not tawkin about cigarettes."

Dom slaps the packs of cigs out of his hand and reaches out to grab him, pulling him in by his shirt. He reaches behind him and pulls out the gun, sticking the barrel down his throat.

"I'm tawkin bout my fuckin brother. I want my fuckin brother!"

Branden eyes turn into shock and fear as Dom presses the muzzle of the gun into the roof of his mouth.

"You fuckin mutilated'im. Metallic flakes and wooden splinters were found inches under'is skin. You fuckin tortured'im. He was found wit over thirty broken bones, some broken so bad, they pierced'is lungs and organs and others protrudin outta'is skin. You broke'is face so bad, we had to have a closed casket funeral. I couldn't even look at my baby brother to say goodbye to'im. You fuckin monster. Fuck you!"

Dom shoves Branden to his knees, cocks the gun and walks him to the river until his body is leaning over the river, the water unusually high for early December.

"Rot in hell!"

Dom is holding Branden by the collar of his shirt as he pulls the trigger, sending a bullet through his brain, feeling his body slump dead in his hand. Tears begin to run down Dom's face. But it doesn't matter. He just keeps pulling the trigger. Screaming and crying and pulling it and pulling it until the bullets stop and all Dom hears are the clicks of the hammer hitting the empty gun.

With tears flowing, Dom lets go of Branden, watching his body fall off the edge of the trail and into the water. He looks down at his hands, covered in blood from Branden's brain leakage.

He sits down on the trail and pulls out his phone, his bloodied, shaking fingers barely able to dial the numbers.

'Nine one one, what's your emergency?'

'There's been a murder near the Pennypack Bridge.'

'Okay sir, what's your name?'

'Dominic Mooney.'

'Okay Mr. Mooney, what happened?'

'I . . . I killed him.'

Dom hangs up the phone and lets go of it, the blood-stained phone falling to the ground. He lays his head back on the asphalt trail and curls into a ball, holding onto the gun like a stuffed animal, the blood on his hands staining his face and shirt.

Dom looks at the glistening night sky, the moon his only friend. He feels a rock under his leg and moves, only for it to return as he rolls back to his side. He looks down to find a stray bullet is in his pocket, not a rock.

He pulls it out of his pocket, sitting up and staring at the silver casing, glistening in the moonlight, with the brown lead bullet sitting atop of the casing like a king on a throne. He releases the cylinder, watching it fall from the side, staring at the empty casings. He pushes back the ejector rod and watches the six gold-tinted casings fall from the gun. Through tear-filled eyes, he stares at the muzzle, now covered in blood and brain matter. With the faint smell of gunpowder in the air, he loads the bullet into the cylinder and whips it shut. He feels his hand move the muzzle of the pistol towards his left temple and gently press against it, closing his eyes as his finger slowly moves its way onto the trigger.

Suddenly, all Dom sees are his parent's faces.

The look of his mother's face when she leaned over and kissed the top of the casket in the aisle at the funeral.

The look of his father's face when he just stood over the grave, not moving. Face expressionless but tears falling like a gentle waterfall down his saddened cheeks.

Dom moves the muzzle away from his temple and sits up, the grip of the gun soaked in blood. He looks at the gun, his bloody handprint staring back at him. He releases the cylinder and pushes the rod back, ejecting the round. He stares at it for a moment and tosses it into the river, the bullet flickering in the moonlight for a moment.

He walks towards the exit of the trails from under the bridge, the cop sirens ringing about the dark December night. He sees the flashlights of the police shining on the ground as they approach him.

He whips the cylinder shut, lays the gun on the ground, walks back a few feet, places his hands on his head and gets to his knees. The cops approach the teen, yelling commands but the mood turns somber as they see him kneeling, covered in blood and crying uncontrollably.

All that Dom can think about is what he said to his baby brother at the funeral, as he stares out the window of the cop car.

I did it Donny. I did it baby brother. I'll always have your back.

Always.

X

Lissy and her parents are all sitting on the couch, eyes glued to the television. Their living room table is littered with empty plates and bowls of chips, salsa, wings, popcorn and more. A few minutes prior, the rookie kicker just drilled a field goal, giving them the lead by eight. Mr. Mooney stares at the television, donning a backwards Birds cap and a throwback Cunningham jersey.

"Come on. Come on. Come on!"

He moves his sight from the game to the clock. Second and ten. Nine seconds left. Everyone is standing on their toes, bouncing up and down with excitement bursting from their veins. Mr. Mooney reaches down and grabs his water bottle, taking a swig of it and wiping his brow of the sweat.

"HIKE!"

They snap the ball back and the quarterback is shuffling in place. Suddenly, a sea of green races across the screen and almost sacks him. He races to the outside and launches the ball, the clock running down to zero as it flies through the air at blistering speeds. It reaches the apex and starts coming back to Earth even faster than before. Blurs of green and white batter the television screen, the pigskin getting lost in the tsunami of bodies. Finally, after a second that felt like a lifetime, the ball pops out and falls to the field. Mr. Mooney holds his breath, afraid to speak, in fear of a flag being thrown. After a few seconds, the announcers confirms his suspicions.

"THE PHILADELPHIA EAGLES ARE SUPER BOWL CHAMPIONS!"

Screams of joy erupt from the Mooney household, with cheers and fireworks echoing through the streets and skies of Northeast Philadelphia and all of the City of Brotherly Love. Tears of joy begin streaming down Mr. Mooney's face. He looks around the living room in joy, his eyes becoming fixed on the pictures of his two sons, whose school photos are hanging on the living room wall next to the stairs. His joy turns to sadness. But his sadness becomes joy as he walks outside of the house and looks up at the twilight-blue sky, splattered with stars.

"We did it boys. It finally happened."

His eyes become overwhelmed with tears as he utters a sentence through choked words.

"Hey Donny. . .Thanks for tawkin to the Man Upstairs for us."

He remained outside for a few minutes, the moon his only friend and as his eyes remained fixed on the stars, he could've sworn he saw two of them sparkle.

I love you both.

Never forget it.

Made in the USA
Middletown, DE
02 March 2021